WITHDRAWN

D1161856

THE JUDGE'S STORY

THE
JUDGE'S STORY

BY
CHARLES MORGAN

"There is an inmost centre in us all,
Where truth abides in fulness. . . ."
BROWNING, *Paracelsus*

"Thou torturest me, Tubal: it was my turquoise; I had it
of Leah when I was a bachelor: I would not have given it
for a wilderness of monkeys."
SHAKESPEARE, *The Merchant of Venice*, III, i

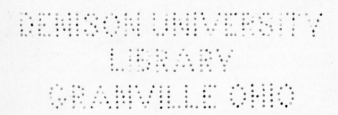

DENISON UNIVERSITY
LIBRARY
GRANVILLE OHIO

THE MACMILLAN COMPANY
NEW YORK · 1947

COPYRIGHT, 1946, 1947, BY CHARLES MORGAN

All rights reserved—no part of this book may be
reproduced in any form without permission in
writing from the publisher, except by a reviewer
who wishes to quote brief passages in connection
with a review written for inclusion in magazine
or newspaper.

PRINTED IN THE UNITED STATES OF AMERICA

Second printing.

823
M82j

DENISON UNIVERSITY
LIBRARY
GRANVILLE OHIO

117627

To
SHIRLEY MORGAN

**HER FATHER DEDICATES
THIS STORY**

12-15-44 mccc 2⁰⁰

THE JUDGE'S STORY

1

At the Royal Automobile Club, to which he belonged for the sake of its swimming-bath and because it was near to Rodd's, Severidge had swum four lengths and eaten four sandwiches. This energetic and frugal process had been accurately timed. It was not his habit to be either early or late. No timepiece ever contradicted him unless it was wrong, and when he looked inquiringly at the post-office clock at the bottom of St. James's, it replied obediently: "Two-thirteen". At a quarter past, he would be on the steps of Rodd's. In that ancient club, he would drink a glass of brown sherry and play one rubber of bridge. From three-fifteen his car would be waiting for him. At three-forty-five or earlier he would be back in the chairman's room of Combined Metallurgical Industries—his first afternoon appointment, with Haslip of the Treasury, was at three-fifty—and would work there until he drove back to South Street to dress for dinner.

He reviewed his evening engagements. Guests arriving eight-thirty. Reach South Street, seven-forty-five. Downstairs again, eight-ten. Twenty minutes for personal letters: one to his sister about her tiresome boy; one to the old lady in Scotland who had a manuscript of Cennini's Treatise, dated 1431, six years earlier than the Vatican copy—and *illustrated*. Severidge grinned. He had examined those illustrations when the manuscript was on loan at the Fifteenth Century Italian Exhibition that spring and knew what they were worth. To his first letter, composed and typed by his secretary, the old lady had replied that she was "astonished" by his suggestion; she had no "desire or intention" to sell; nor did she wish to have correspondence with "dealers". Hence the need of a personal letter in his own hand. She'd sell in the end. Everything was for sale. Meanwhile he was amused by her resistance, as he was by the resistance of younger women in other matters. He liked them high-mettled. He liked a siege. Only proved his point in the end.

Looking ahead of him, as he approached Rodd's, he saw the Judge come out of the club and turn down the hill towards him. In a moment they would meet, and Severidge prepared his smile and his bit of banter. Gaskony had been retired from the Bench two years. Must be getting on. But these Victorians—the hard-working ones who had had their own way to make and neither the time nor the means to go raffish in the 'nineties—wore well. Gaskony, stepping down St. James's in the July sunshine, shone with health and quiet assurance. Hooked on his left arm was a neatly furled umbrella; in that hand a little package in brown paper was held almost proudly, as though he were a boy who had been out shopping. In his other hand, easily swinging, was his hat, which, no doubt, he would put on presently; meanwhile, he was sunning himself, his long grey head cocked a little at the blue sky, his shoulders braced, his old, well-polished black boots glinting as he came.

"Well, Judge, you're very brisk this afternoon."

Gaskony came down benignly out of the sky. "Ah, Severidge, going in for your rubber?"

"Turn back and join us."

"Bless my soul," said Gaskony, "where's my hat?" and, noticing it in his hand, he put it on. Then he smiled. "Stakes too high," he said. "I'm an old fogey, not a Regency buck." His eyes twinkled at Severidge. "You must have been a member of the Hell Fire Club in a previous existence. Besides, my game's whist—or was a bit."

"We'll play whist," Severidge volunteered with good humour. "A glass of sherry, a game of whist, very civilized on a summer afternoon. My car will be here at three-fifteen. I can put you on your way. Come," and he would have taken the Judge's arm.

But Gaskony seemed not to notice the movement. His elbows

clipped his sides. Why he wants my company I don't know, he thought, but he always does, though he don't like me. Odd.

"No good to me, unfortunately. I'm going down to Surrey to see my daughter—the girl I told you of once; not my daughter, my ward."

"Vivien," Severidge put in, quick as lightning, referring to the infallible card-index of his mind. "Vivien . . . wait, don't tell me . . . Vivien Brown? Am I right? Brown. That's why I missed it for a moment. It's always the uncommon names that jump up easiest."

"You're an astonishing chap," said Gaskony. "How do you remember that? I can't have mentioned the name more than once in your hearing."

Severidge patted the Judge's forearm. "Once is enough, or ought to be. I don't forget. You met her mother, didn't you, in a bookshop? . . . Surely, a bookshop in Chancery Lane? . . . And didn't the mother die when the girl was born? And the father soon after? A moving story, I thought. Impressed itself on my mind. I remember things, you know, by the places where I heard them. It was in my yacht coming up from the Aegean, on deck one night. I was staring out to sea while you were telling that tale; the moon was up, and I imagined that dark little bookshop. That's what planted 'Chancery Lane' in my memory. We made Corfu next day."

"I remember well, a glorious night," Gaskony answered, wondering why he had told even a part of Vivien's story to this man of all men.

"And how is she?"

"Well, thank you. . . . But she's not Brown any more. Married just before our voyage together. Your infernal memory has played you false on that. Married to young Henry Lerrick. Member of Rodd's. I put him up. Do you know him?"

"Indeed I do. Cheerful young man, I thought. If his bridge is any evidence of his ability in other things, he ought to go far. I'll ask them to dine one night in South Street."

There was nothing to say except: "That would be good of

you," and Gaskony said it. "Well," he added, "I shall be missing my train."

At that Severidge's eye lighted on the little package. "You look like a young man come out of a jeweller's. Is it a birthday?"

The Judge was taken aback. His fingers tightened on the package. "Well, yes," he said,—"and no."

2

SEVERIDGE, he had noticed, always had the effect upon him—
a devilish uncomfortable effect—of drawing him out. Chiefly,
perhaps, because he wished so little to be drawn out by him
and was therefore the more anxious not to be stand-offish.
Moreover, he was under the obligation of that voyage in the
Aegean, undertaken within a couple of months of his retiring
from the Bench, during which no one could have had a more
generous and forbearing host. It had been the year of Vivien's
marriage; young Lerrick had carried her off to Italy in the
spring; and the Judge, without her and without his Court to
go to, had been at a loose end. He had a book to write, that
was true; *his* book, which in his mind he called *The Athenian*.
All his life he had been waiting to write it and preparing for it;
in a sense, it was his life, from which everything else, the Bar,
the Bench, had been a diversion; and when he retired from the
Bench, the way was clear, he had his chance. But he had been
tired. All that business with young Lerrick had tried him.
It hadn't been easy at first to make himself understand that
when Vivien looked at the boy with fixed eyes or tautened at
the sound of his slap-dash, lilting voice, it was natural, it meant
only that she was alive and happy and human and hungrily in
love. The courtship with its comings and goings, cars at all
hours, telephones, telegrams, quick breathings, starings from the
window, silences, raptures, sudden breathless confidences—this
had tried him. When the engagement was firm, he had made
arrangements to sell the little manor-house where Vivien had
lived with him since she was a child, for henceforward he
would be pensioned, he must cut down expenses; and Vivien

shouldn't go to her marriage penniless, she must have enough for her clothes and her fal-lals, though young Lerrick, who was well enough off if he went steady, must not be given the idea, while he was unproven, that there was money of his wife's to burn. To settle this, to have new shelves built into his flat in the Temple, to move his books and his *Athenian* material, to docket his country furniture and his garden stuff for the auctioneers; finally, with the help of Mrs. Partridge, his house-keeper, and the bride's old nurse, Lou, who came back for the occasion, to arrange the wedding itself, and attend it, and wave good-bye with the feel of Vivien's quick kiss on his cheek—well, it had thrown him out of gear for *The Athenian*.

"And what are you going to do, Judge?" Severidge had asked across the oval table at Rodd's.

"Give mine enemy a chance."

"Write a book? About what?"

"Periclean Athens. But not yet. I need a holiday. Besides, I must go to Athens again."

Severidge had said: "That's easy. Two at a blow. Holiday and Athens. Come in my yacht."

Intuition had warned Gaskony, and he had answered: "Thank you, Severidge, that's good of you, but it sounds too grand for me. I should want to shut myself up in libraries and poke about in holes and corners. I should spoil your party."

"But, my dear Judge," Severidge had answered, "there isn't a party. The thing came into my head just sixty seconds ago. The yacht's laid up but I'll recommission her. No one but our-selves. To-day three weeks? You can poke about as much as you like."

So it had happened two years ago, in the early summer of Thirty-Two; and the Judge remembered it keenly, every word as it was spoken, and the look in Severidge's eye—the theatrical-*generalissimo* look which seemed to say: Look at me! How drastic and powerful I am. For me the heavens fall. I nod, and time stands still.

That voyage had been a link between them ever since, and bless me, thought the Judge as he turned half-right out of the

Mall and glanced up at Queen Victoria's statue, I can't complain. Severidge is tiresome sometimes; has a way of buttonholing you; makes me feel like the old monk—what's his name?
—who, when he looked up from his desk to see the view, always found a little Devil lookin' in at the window; but that voyage was worth while if ever a voyage was. Sunshine, blue skies, the drive up to Delphi; eagles, as you looked across the valley, floating in the air at the level of your nose; and, in the yacht herself, hard reading, docketing notes, Severidge doing his physical jerks regular as clockwork, a quiet, abstemious life for all its comforts, and in the evenings on deck a glass of brandy, a good cigar and the islands drifting by with the moon on them, like snow. And the material I got for my *Athenian!* Not material only but the feel of it.

He began to wonder whether he had, in the same sense, the feel of it now. Well, naturally he hadn't; this was Victoria Station, not the Acropolis; but the feel would come back to him when he began to write—when he said to himself at last: there, my material is complete, and shook off Rodd's and his playgoing, and his journeys to see Vivien and his visits to Oxford and his little dinners in the Temple and all the rest of it, and became himself and began to write.

Soon, he said, as he walked on to the platform. Soon it must be, he repeated, as he settled himself into his corner seat, the years run on; but that voyage put me on a new track, the material isn't complete yet, and I am not idle, I peg away. Say another six months or so. Or nine months. This winter in London; then, next spring, I could go away. Real peace. No more obligations. No more engagements. An open calendar. My own life that I've wanted since I was eighteen. Forty-eight years. For me, the good life. In nine months, sooner perhaps, the material will be complete.

He glanced over his left shoulder at the suburbs streaming past. Severidge's face looked in at the window and said: It's complete now. You know it is. And then Severidge said: Holiday and Athens. Come again in my yacht.

Leave me alone! the Judge murmured within him, shaping

the words with his lips. He put the jeweller's package into the hat which stood on the seat beside him. Then, having observed that the lady opposite had rosy cheeks—and God did all, or I'm a Dutchman—he picked up the afternoon edition of his evening paper and looked at the cricket scores. Severidge was supposed to have an interest in that paper. Had he? A controlling interest? People chattered nonsense about such things. Because a man was rich he was said to have a finger in every pie.

Gaskony blinked, rustled his newspaper, and put behind him the thought of Severidge, the temptations of the Aegean. . . . Vivien, he reflected, was one of the few women on earth who wasn't bored by cricket. Time they went to Lord's together. Young Lerrick would take her to the Eton and Harrow match, being an Etonian. Well, he could; Gaskony didn't care, being a Wykehamist. He dropped the newspaper and began to wonder what an Athenian boy would have made of cricket. Too static, presumably. Plato, certainly, would have had none of it; not military enough for him by a long chalk; there was a passage in the *Laws* in which it was clear that he wouldn't have allowed even foot-races except in full armour; but Plato, in that mood, was a curmudgeon, more Spartan than Athenian, and you had to make allowances for him. You had to remember—

"Croydon? Yes, indeed. Croydon's my station." Hat, parcel, gloves, everything. Off hat. "Thank'ee, ma'am. Most good of you to remind me."

"Your umbrella too," said the lady, handing it out.

"Ah! Thank'ee so well. Thank'ee kindly."

He watched the train draw out. He had liked the little veil half-way to the tip of her nose. Veils, presumably, were coming in again, though he hadn't seen Vivien wearing one. . . . And you had to remember, he thought as he walked up the slope towards the ticket-barrier, that almost any form of exercise that could be taught, that could be specialized in, would have appealed to Athenian youth. A paidotribes, with his class of javelin-throwers, couldn't have been unlike a professional at the nets, they as keen as mustard and he—as solemn as a judge.

3

OUTSIDE the station he found a taxi that would drive him through Croydon and its immediate suburbs into Hadscombe, which the taxi-driver called "the country". Though far from being country now, it still contained what had once been the country houses of City merchants and flourishing professional men, and among them was the Red House, which had belonged to Henry Lerrick's father. Not that Bright, Lerrick had ever been one of the great firms of solicitors if you reckoned by the volume of its commercial business; it had always been mainly of the solid family kind; but it had flourished in its own way, and many a comfortable brief had Gaskony had from Tom Lerrick. When Bright died, Henry was already in the firm. Then Tom went also, and Henry had held on alone.

Any amount of confidence, quick, too, plenty of brains, good manners and a general air of all's-well-with-the-world that made private clients, particularly women, feel comfortable. Fresh curtains, white telephones, flowers on the table and all that. No harm in it; good perhaps. The firm had a sound reputation, though a bit lightweight one might say, and it must be doing well enough or Henry couldn't afford to live as he did. Still, why didn't he take a partner? There always had been two, three at one time, and, if business was expanding, there ought to be ample room for a second now.

And the Red House, which had been all very well for Tom when domestic servants and gardeners were two-a-penny, was a white elephant for a young couple nowadays. Bound to be. Two hot-houses, two tennis-lawns, garage, cottage, twelve bedrooms, five servants indoors and extra help on occasions—and now Henry was always chattering of a swimming-pool. Too much. Out of proportion to the times. That fellow Hitler shooting up Roehm in Munich. A "purge" they called it—as if the President of the United States should sally forth from the White House with a troop of gunmen and murder half the Senate overnight. No time to build swimming-pools!

When he arrived before its porch, the Judge gave the Red House such a look as he might have given to a woman who wore too much jewellery. He paid the taxi and rang the bell. Even if they could afford it, much better put away for a rainy day. He would say so again to Vivien. And what would happen if they had a nursery?—not that it looked as if they had enough sense. Anyhow, on that subject he wouldn't comment; being a bachelor put him out of court. But what would happen if there were a war? Even the young couldn't fend that off by saying it was "unthinkable".

As he rang the bell again, the door opened. He braced himself to be received by Kingsley, the parlour-maid, an episcopal woman whom Henry always spoke of as Bath and Wells; but it was Kathleen, the Irish girl, who welcomed him, the set of her apron and "a cuff neglectful" pleasantly explaining her delay.

Under her smile, he put off the judicial air appropriate to Kingsley. "Well, Kathleen, how are you all? Mistress at home?"

"Not yet, Sir William, but she soon will be. If you were to come first, she said, you were to be put in the garden."

"But you weren't expecting me?"

"No, Sir William, not expecting. But we are always hoping you will come."

"That's what we English call blarney, Kathleen."

"Yes, Sir William."

"And though we may like it, we're not taken in."

"Oh no, Sir William. Nor are we. It's just a way of speaking."

Which explains, Gaskony thought, why the Irish are sometimes the best advocates and always the best witnesses in the world; they can retract anything without contradicting themselves; and he followed her across the hall and through the library—"a winning wave, deserving note, in the tempestuous petticoat". On the terrace, where a table was already laid for tea, she installed him in a wicker armchair. Should she make tea now? "N—no," he replied thirstily, "better wait for the mistress," but he lifted the cover of a dish to find beneath it cucumber sandwiches.

"Kathleen," he said, "did you ever see the play that begins with the man who ate all the cucumber sandwiches before tea began?"

"No, Sir William, never."

"You should. *The Importance of Being Earnest*. Written by a countryman of yours."

Within a few minutes of her vanishing, Kathleen returned with a cup of tea in her hand. "Out of our own pot," she explained, "just to be passing the time. Is it too strong?"

He took it gratefully: "Can't be too strong."

Left alone, with the hot stuff flowing down inside him, he looked out over the edge of the cup at the sloping lawn and the flower-beds, a little surprised as he always was when, being solitary, he returned to a sense of his origins and found himself established in the midst of prosperity. His first home had had a little dusty lawn, but there had been evergreens in the midst of it and palings at the edge. He and his brother Dick, and Phil Brown too when he came to stay, used to carry their books on to the lawn and work there on hot mornings, taking no notice of the tradesmen's carts and pretending not to hear the neighbours who looked over the palings and said: "Hullo, working again?" When the gate clicked during his father's consulting hours and a patient came up the gravel and rang the Surgery bell, the evergreens gave shelter to the studious group on the lawn, but their concentration wasn't perfect; at the sound of a footstep on the gravel and of a voice saying: "Is the doctor in?" Dick's head would come up sometimes from his Greek text and he would yawn—the yawn of hunger, not of sleepiness; for, until the evening meal, even food had been scanty at home; everything had been cut down to pay for books and education, so rigid had been their father's ambition for his sons. Would he have been satisfied now, if he had lived? Perhaps: Dick, the Provost of St. Peter's at Oxford—that would have pleased Father, Gaskony thought; and as for myself? A Judge of the High Court—yes, that is something; but Father wouldn't have liked it when I retired. "Who knows, Will?" Father used to say. "Work hard, my boy, there are great prizes at the Bar. Some day you might be Lord Chief Justice. You might be Lord Chancellor. You have the brains. It's only a question of putting your heart into the race, every minute and every second of it, and keeping your eyes on the tape. And, if you take my advice, don't marry—or don't marry young. Marriage is like a dead body tied to a poor man."

Well, said the Judge to himself, my heart wasn't in the Bar—that's the long and short of it; I ought to have been a writer and dead poor, like Phil Brown; and as for marriage—his eyebrows went up—fate decided against that, no wise discretion of mine, God knows. . . . I ought to have been a writer, he repeated. Or is that a fond delusion? Do men with a real vocation neglect it? If they neglect it, isn't that a proof that the vocation itself was what Vivien would call "phoney"? He wondered whether his young-man verses had been as good as he had thought they were, and was troubled by an old suspicion, which brought a wry smile to his lips, that his Greek verses had always been better than his English. . . . And anyway, he thought, setting down his cup and helping himself to a cucumber sandwich, life isn't over yet. There's still my *Athenian* to be written. Soon I shall begin to write. Six months. Nine months. Soon it must be, very soon now.

The sun was warm on his hands, though his face was in the shade, and he began to nod in the balmy scent of that July day, almost knowing in his heart that his *Athenian* would never be written.

> The world is too much with us; late and soon,
> Getting and spending, we lay waste our powers:

—Julia's favourite sonnet.

"And what are you doing there, Gasky?" Julia's voice asked beside him, and he opened his eyes to see Vivien, in a flowered cotton frock, and to feel her hand on his shoulder, forbidding him to rise. But he rose and kissed her so that she might know he wasn't old and hadn't been asleep.

"Doing?" he said. "I was just saying over your dear mother's favourite sonnet."

"Oh, that one!" she answered. " 'Or hear old Triton blow his wreathèd horn'?" and she smiled, setting down the parcels she had in her arms.

"Well," he exclaimed, "what's wrong with that? It's a magnificent sonnet."

"I know. I'm not denying it," she said. "It's only that 'old Triton' blowing—yes, Kathleen, thank you, put it there. And do you think you could get the flame under the kettle to light?" Then she turned to him again. "How nice to see you, Gasky. Have you been waiting long for your tea?"

"I haven't been waiting at all, my dear. Kathleen gave me a cup. Real strong kitchen tea. Stood my spoon up in it."

4

Though he had been nodding when she came, it did not enter Vivien's mind to think of her guardian as an old man. His hair was glossy still, and the warm, clean colour of his cheeks made a decoration of the brisk white brushed up from his forehead and above his ears. His movement was brisk, too; his smile as lively and his voice as firm as they had been when he had told her stories in her childhood. She enjoyed his company; it amused her and it made her feel safe. Whether even Victorian solidity could stand up to the world that was coming, she often doubted in theory; but she did not doubt in practice that, as long as Gasky was alive, he would be as he always had been—for her, life's ultimate guarantee; always on her side whatever scrape she got into; always with a margin; the one certain thing on earth—unchanging, unanxious, never on edge.

"Before I forget, Vivien—just to put you on the *qui vive*— I think I may have done you and your Henry a good turn on the way down here."

"Thank heaven for that. We need it."

"What does that mean?"

She hesitated. The phrase had slipped out. "Mean?" she said, recovering herself. "Nothing. Only that a little luck is always welcome."

"Are you out of luck?"

"Not particularly. But tell me: how did you do us a good turn?"

"By mistake, I confess. I met Severidge."

She shook her head. "Who is he?"

Gaskony laughed with delight. "Say that again, Vivien!"

"Sorry," she said. "Honestly, I've never heard of him."

"Ever heard of Rockefeller?"

"Well yes, by distant report. But very distant. Is Severidge as rich as that?"

"No, my dear, probably not. But he *is* C.M.I." When this, too, missed fire, he rubbed his cheek as a mark of extreme satisfaction. "Now," he said, "I know at last that I brought you up properly. I used to wonder sometimes. Too secluded, perhaps, I thought. But if you have reached the age of twenty-seven without ever having heard of Combined Metallurgical Industries, I am justified."

She smiled. "Now sophisticate me."

"Well," he said, "Severidge is a queer man, but an interesting one. Surely I've talked to you about him before? It was in his yacht I went to Greece, the year you were married."

"Oh," she answered, "that man!"

"As you say, that man. But the fact that he took me to Greece isn't his only title to distinction, and he's going to invite you and Henry to dine."

"Do we go?"

"I expect so."

"Why, if you dislike him? You do, don't you?"

"Dislike? . . . Mm—no. I wouldn't say 'dislike'. 'Pon my soul, Vivien, I should rather like you to dine with him. He seems to have taken to Henry a bit at the club and, from a professional point of view, it's an acquaintance worth cultivating. Pretty big crumbs fall from that rich man's table. But that's Henry's concern. I should like you to go because I'd dearly love to hear what you make of the chap. Women make good guesses sometimes, and he beats me."

"As a judge," she began to tease him, "with your experience of human nature——"

"Ah!" he exclaimed, "as a judge, yes. But no one's a judge in his own case, and this *is* my case. Any link he can forge with me, you can bet your bottom dollar he will forge it. This notion of asking you and Henry to dine in South Street is partly that. He may ask me on that occasion or he may not;

depends on his technique; but if he does he'll talk *at* me, and if he doesn't—you mark my words—he'll talk about me."

"All the symptoms of love!" Vivien said.

"All the symptoms of—not love, my dear."

"Hatred?"

"Oh no, I think not. Why do you say that? Oh no, I think not."

Alarm in his tone made her aware that his mind was troubled, and she looked at him at first with surprise—he was ordinarily so unruffled—then with an affection that eclipsed her own anxieties. When by mistake she had said that she and Henry "needed" a good turn, Gasky had let it pass; and he wouldn't have let it pass if this man Severidge hadn't been pretty heavy on his mind.

"What is it, Gasky?" she asked.

He met her eyes with so sharp a turn of the head that she thought for a moment he intended to ride away from the subject. Indeed he began to ride away from it. "Nothing," he said, "nothing, of course, to worry about." Then he took her hand for a moment, held it, let it go, and said: "Well, why shouldn't the old sometimes take counsel of the young? It's pretty vague, my dear, but it troubles me just for that reason. Severidge is always bobbing up. It's not only in Rodd's that I meet him. If I walk down St. James's, there he is, walking up it. If I go to dine in a private house—Mrs. Langferry's last Thursday, the Aldrings' the week before—there he is among the guests, as genial and friendly as you please, but always drawing the conversation on to me. Like a spotlight. Now I've known Kate Langferry ten years and Arthur Aldring half my life, but, for both of them, Severidge was a new acquaintance. 'How did you get to know him?' I asked Kate, and she said: 'By chance as one does, and then somehow we spoke of you. Mr. Severidge spoke so warmly of you that I thought it would be a good party.' Arthur said much the same. And they were quite right. It did make a good party. He's not a selfish talker. He draws me out. Almost defers to me—what's the word they use in the music-halls?"

" 'Feed'?"

"That's it: he 'feeds' me with questions—just the questions, too, that I can answer best. Sometimes a point of law, the kind of point that interests a general company. Sometimes history, and by Jove he's well enough read to know what questions to ask. Sometimes connoisseurship—porcelain, glass, old manuscripts—though he knows much more about that than I do; he's a great collector; spends a fortune on it, though I can never make out *what* he collects, what his central motive is, so to speak. . . . But most often what he makes me talk about is my own real subject."

"Greece? That's natural enough, Gasky, seeing that you went on that voyage together," Vivien said. "I expect you talked of nothing else. And you do talk well about it. Most people do about the love of their life."

He smiled at the compliment, waving it away with a little flourish of his tea-spoon. "That may be, Vivien." Then he took a deep breath and continued: "But I haven't really told you. All that—meeting him everywhere, finding him under my feet, if I may put it so—all that isn't what worries me."

She said nothing and waited until at last he came out with: "What worries me is that he's so often in my thoughts."

"Do you mean you dream about him?"

"No, oddly enough I don't. . . . In my waking thoughts. It makes me feel as if he were trying to get at me in some way. Obviously it isn't that he wants anything from me——"

"Unless friendship, perhaps," Vivien suggested. "Perhaps he's a lonely man—like a stray dog that comes sidling up to you."

The Judge shook his head. "This," he said, "isn't a stray dog. Oh no—you look at his eyes." Then he resumed his course at the point at which she had interrupted him. "It's not that he wants anything *from* me, but that——" He paused helplessly, feeling not so much for words as for clear thought to be put into words.

"Is it," she said when she had given him time and he was still silent, "is it that he wants to do something *to* you!"

He gazed at her. "What do you mean? Hurt me in some way?"

"Change you in some way. There are people like that. Not bad people necessarily. I remember them at school. There was a girl there who—you remember that I was passionately keen about music; it was a kind of religion; I worked and worked at it—and that girl's one idea was to stop me practising, to lead me into doing something else. And she was fond of me. She wasn't bad. . . . There really are people like that. Sometimes they want to 'reform' you. Sometimes they want—according to their lights, their own lights—to lift you up when you're down, and sometimes to pull you down when you're up. But in the one case it isn't kindness and in the other case it isn't jealousy. It's a desire to change people, to—to prevent them from being true to themselves."

"That sounds pretty devilish."

"Well, no," she said, "not always. It may be no worse than the habit of dressing a dog up in ribbons and teaching him tricks—just for the pleasure of seeing him behave *not* like a dog. . . . Which I happen to hate, but perfectly pleasant people do it. They say the dog enjoys it, and probably they are right. Dogs do enjoy showing off. We too, I expect."

"Phew!" said Gaskony, "that's a hard saying. . . . Do we enjoy not being true to ourselves? Perhaps we do, God help us."

Vivien hesitated before so much seriousness and let her eyes wander over the sunlit garden. Then, with the sharpness of tone in which the young make themselves say difficult things, she said: "Anyhow, I think that's what temptation means—the really black temptation. Isn't it, Gasky? I mean, isn't that what the whole story comes to?"

"What story? Paradise Lost?"

"I meant the other one. 'Get thee behind me, Satan.'"

But he, being of the older, the urbane generation, would not allow conversation with ladies to strike too far below the surface without an attempt smilingly to rescue it. "Bless me, Vivien," he said, "you are casting my poor friend Severidge for a very invidious part. He hasn't a cloven hoof."

"May be," she answered.

"Besides—temptation?—tempting me to be untrue to myself? In what way? What is 'true to myself' and what 'untrue'?"

She smiled at him. "You *are* 'taking counsel of the young' this afternoon, Gasky! If I had asked you that question, I know what you would have said: that I alone could answer it."

He shrugged his shoulders. "So be it."

For a little while he was still, not perceptibly breathing, and slowly tumult died. Then, the question banished, or almost banished, from thought like a drum-beat gone down over a hill, he said: "Ha! . . . well . . . so be it," and stretched his hand down beside his chair and pulled up his parcel: something solid, something to catch hold of.

"For me?" Vivien said. "It's not my birthday."

"Your mother's. A little diamond clip. Wear it on your blouse. Are they called blouses? Pretty, I thought. . . . Then there's this. Something for small extras. Five'pun note." He fished it out, neatly folded, from his waistcoat pocket.

While she kissed him and thanked him, her mind was saying: Now, I can't do what Henry told me. After that, I *can't* ask him for money. It was a relief. As she put on the clip, she said: "Did he ever know Mother?"

"Who?"

"Mr. Severidge."

"Good Lord, no. I have only known him myself five or six years and she died—how old are you?"

"Twenty-seven."

"Twenty-seven years ago. He must have been still in his 'teens. Certainly he didn't know her. Different period altogether. Why should you ask?"

If she had answered truly, she might have said she had often found that what deeply troubled or delighted him was connected with his love for her mother; but she did not answer now; he gave her no chance. He didn't wish to talk of Severidge. The drum-beat had gone down over the hill and he wouldn't have it returning.

"There's something else I want to talk to you about," he said.

"Better to you, before Henry comes back. By the bye, when do you expect him?"

"Early. Any time now. He has to get up some wine and decant the port. There's a party this evening."

"A big one?"

"No. Ten—including us."

"Too many, Vivien. Too big."

"We go out a lot, you know. One has to return hospitality."

"Certainly. Simple hospitality. Within one's means. But this—" He spread out his arms to include the Red House and all its works. "Why so grand, Vivien? That's what I wanted to talk to you about. Oh, I dare say you can afford it. Henry always says you can; he ought to know; as far as pounds, shillings and pence are concerned, it's none of my business. But it's not so much a question of cash, as I see it; it's a question of scale—of what's appropriate. When I started in life, young married people—even when they were comfortably off—began modestly. Big entertainment wasn't expected of you—of landowners and merchants and so on, I dare say, but not of a young professional man with his way to make. No one thought any better of him for throwing his money about. But here you are, burdened with a house four sizes too big for you, plus entertaining in expensive restaurants, plus theatres, suppers, races, two cars, no children—bless my soul, I don't see what you get out of it! And if I say so to Henry, he just smiles as if he were the Bank of England and says: 'Don't you worry, Gasky. It's quite all right. Nowadays money makes money. It's all a question of prestige.' That may be true if your business is a gambling one—buying on credit and selling on differences—but it's not true of a family lawyer. Money don't make money for him. That's not how prestige comes. It's how to make the big men look down their noses while they drink your champagne."

As she listened, her fingers tight on the arms of her chair, all her fears agreed with him. For her it was not only what he called it—"a question of scale"; it was a question of cash as well; and she knew that the moment was coming at which, if she was to do what Henry wished, she must let her guardian understand that they needed money. But how much? And how desperately? Five hundred pounds to tide them over? More, perhaps. Perhaps even a thousand. She didn't know. Henry had never told her. His moods changed so fast. At one moment it was: "Darling, don't you worry. Next month it will be all right," but at another he would say: "My God, this place eats money. Even when we *aren't* spending, the expenditure goes on, like a leak in a tank—rates, taxes, mortgage, heat, light, wages." And once he had frightened her. He had given her a fur coat for Christmas, and she had looked, without speaking it, her dread of the extravagance. "Anyhow," he had said, "if it's yours, the rats can't get at it. You aren't responsible for my debts." But in the spring she had fought her battle and won it. Henry had agreed to cut drastically, and be rid of the house. In return she had promised to "keep a face on it" meanwhile. "It's no good saving halfpence," he had said. "The big cut" had for him the glorious advantage of sparing them the need to cheesepare; and when they had gone off together to the house-agent's and the Red House was "on the market", a great weight was lifted from their minds. They had been happy again and had given a party to celebrate their freedom, hugging their secret, telling none of their guests what it was they celebrated. Not to tell them had been for Henry a matter of prestige. "But when we do go, we shall have to tell them," she had suggested, but Henry had laughed and kissed her and said it might never come to that after all; he had a feeling that everything would take a turn for the better because she was so beautiful and had persuaded him to be so wise.

She was a little tired sometimes of mothering Henry, of bearing ultimate responsibility in those matters for which, outwardly, he was responsible; but if they were in trouble for money, she reflected, Henry, like a spendthrift child, was certainly a charming person to be in trouble with, and before the Judge had finished his discourse her fears had ebbed. There was a brilliant smile on her lips as she let out the secret:

"As a matter of fact, Gasky, you needn't worry. Not

seriously, I mean—though it's true we are short of money now. But the big cut has been made."

"Oh," he said, "that's new. Don't see much signs of it."

"The house."

"Sold?"

"Not yet, but it's on the market."

"Is it indeed? Since when?"

"April."

"What made Henry decide on that? He always took the other line."

"Well," she said, "it isn't really suitable for us. Young-marrieds like ourselves mostly live right in London or right in the country or both. Henry clung to this, though Hadscombe's almost a suburb, oh—partly, I suppose, because he was born here and likes it, partly because, you know, people *do* come here to us; it's a change, I suppose, from flats and poky little houses with grand addresses, and so it's different, and the garden's lovely at night with fairy-lamps and things, so that you forget it's a suburb. In a way—among the people we know, I mean—the Red House is quite famous. People *do* come."

"I don't doubt it."

"I mean, in a way, from Henry's point of view, it's good for prestige."

"Prestige be damned!" said the Judge. "I beg your pardon, my dear, but you're just echoing him."

"I like the Red House, too," she answered. "We have been happy here. We are very happy, Henry and I."

"Yes, Vivien, I know. I give him marks for that. But Henry's like one of your cocktails. Makes things look rosy for a minute, and then . . . well . . . heaven knows I don't blame you for wanting to stick to this place. Rather a Victorian sentiment I should have thought for young people like you. Still——"

"You forget," she interrupted, "that you brought me up, Gasky."

That pleased him, but he returned to the attack. "But all these reasons for staying," he said, "still hold, don't they?"

"We changed our minds."

"Why? Money?"

"Partly."

"Debts?"

"Yes, I think so. Until we did this."

"Did what?"

"Decided to leave the house."

"But you haven't left it."

"We haven't sold it yet."

"What are you asking for it?"

"Seventeen thousand."

"The deuce you are! Old Tom Lerrick gave six thousand five. You'll never get seventeen or half of seventeen. Listen, Vivien; what does all this mean?" She was puzzled and silent. "With a price like that the house isn't genuinely on the market at all."

This had occurred to her when she and Henry had gone to the house-agent's together, but she had quieted herself with Henry's answer. "But we must have seventeen," she said now, echoing him.

"*Must?* What for?"

"Well, to buy another place, I suppose, and then a bit over."

"How much over? You mean debts?"

"There's the mortgage to pay off, Henry says."

"Nonsense. That could remain. How much loose debts— over and above?"

"Honestly, Gasky, I don't know. Perhaps five hundred."

"Or more?"

"It might be a bit more."

He stood up. "I don't like this," he said.

"But after we've sold the house——"

He broke in on her. "Vivien. Vivien. Screw your head on. At that price you never will. And meanwhile all this runs on—" He stretched out his arms and looked up at the offending house, only to see, coming out of the library, young Henry, as cheerful as a grig.

"Hullo, Gasky. Glad you've been keeping her company."
He put his arm round his wife's shoulder, stooped, and kissed
her. "Darling, we have a new invitation to dine on Tuesday
night. Can we get out of the Brandells'? I had to accept the
new one. Rather important and special."

"May I ask," said Gaskony, "whether you have been winning
at bridge?"

"Fifteen pounds."

"Severidge?"

"In fact it was."

"Talk about me?"

"Yes."

"Oh well, I suppose it's natural enough. I met him going into
Rodd's." There was so much that the Judge wished to say—
of Severidge, of economy, of the Red House and the Munich
murders and the state of the world and swimming-pools—that
he could say none of it. No time. They had guests—eight of
them. It wasn't an evening on which he could invite himself to
dinner. "Look," he said, pulling out his watch, "would you
telephone for a taxi from that garage of yours? I must go if
I'm to catch my train."

Henry said he had not put his own car away. "A glass of
sherry first? Then I'll drive you down. I'd drive you into
London if we hadn't guests coming."

The sherry was dry and clean. The pink of roses and the
tea-kettle's silver laced its golden fires. You couldn't drink a
man's sherry and say: tell me, have you paid for this yet? so
they drank peacefully, chattering of trivial things. Henry
noticed Vivien's new diamond clip and was as grateful for it as
she had been. All the way to the station he talked of her as if
he had fallen in love with her yesterday, and the Judge forgave
him his sins—forgave him the more readily because he thought
that he detected, beneath the talkative gaiety of Henry's
manner, a certain nervous stress. What's wrong? the Judge
thought. The boy's on edge—talking of one thing, thinking of
another. . . . But Henry did not falter. He locked the car, came
into the station, bought a platform ticket and kept the old man

smiling and laughing until the train came in. Only one slip did he make.

"How's the great work?" he asked, intending to please, but Gaskony didn't want to be asked about his *Athenian*. Six months. Nine months. Soon it must be . . . late and soon, getting and spending we lay waste—

"Pretty well, thank'ee," he said, "pretty well," and settled in his corner. Henry provided him with another evening paper, and waved as the train started.

DENISON UNIVERSITY
LIBRARY
GRANVILLE OHIO

5

In the Temple, an island of walled quiet within twenty yards of Fleet Street, Gaskony had a top-floor flat which looked down on to the roof, the courtyard and the trees of Middle Temple Hall. Here, with the assistance of Mrs. Clutterbuck, who came in by day, and of her friend, Mrs. Sullins, who came in to wait "when there was company", he had lived comfortably for twelve years whenever he had been in London, and continuously since Vivien's marriage. Mrs. Clutterbuck suited him, for she was a good cook, a cheerful woman, and a servant who took the long hours with the short; and he suited Mrs. Clutterbuck, for he praised her little prides, dined out continually, was often away, and had a blind eye for the plunder that she carried off in her string bag.

This evening he would dine in and alone. If he had been invited to dinner at Hadscombe, he would have telephoned to Mrs. Clutterbuck. As it was, he climbed the many flights of stairs with a mingled sense of loneliness and satisfaction—of satisfaction because circumstances compelled him to be alone, to settle down to his *Athenian*, and because he knew that, when once he was settled down, the desire for distraction would be lifted from him and he would be happy. The enthusiasm of his student's days would return to him, the glowing assurance that what he did was for him of ultimate value. His thought would burn clear, his whole being would be warmed and illumined by it; he would know with certainty that he was leading the kind of life to which he had been called, and would be inwardly happy, suffused by that sense of fulfilment and innocence which Vivien's mother alone had understood in him.

DENISON UNIVERSITY
LIBRARY

Others had understood the greed of scholarship, the strange acquisitive desire to know; others, again, could sympathize with an ambition to be the author of a memorable book—"how is the great work?" Henry Lerrick asked always; but only Julia had grasped and felt his truth, which did not rest upon the pride either of scholarship or of reputation, but upon the innermost glow of thought itself, a stilled and burning felicity, an incandescence of his otherwise flickering soul. Which all means, he thought with a smile as he entered his flat and saw Mrs. Clutterbuck through the open doorway of her kitchen, that I am like one of those Aladdin lamps we had in the country— at first all flicker and no light; but give it time, leave it alone a little while, turn it up gradually, and suddenly the whole mantle becomes . . .

He went first into his work-room, lined with books, and, in preparation for the night's work, unlocked his *Athenian* filing-cabinets; then, on his way to the living-room, he called out:

"Supper as soon as you like, Mrs. Clutterbuck. No claret. I shall work late to-night. I'll change now into pyjamas and a dressing-gown while you are dishing up."

"Oh, Sir William, I wern't sure whether to make supper or no," said Mrs. Clutterbuck, coming out into the little square hall. "Your brother 'e phoned up an' said 'e was up from Oxford for the night and was comin' round to fetch you out for a the-ater."

"When?" said the Judge.

"He might be at the door any minute now," Mrs. Clutterbuck answered with the dramatic refusal of her kind to calculate time or distance. "I did tell 'im, Sir William, as you would be workin' to-night if you didn't stay down at 'Adscombe, but 'e said nonsense Mrs. Clutterbuck 'e said, you tell the Judge as it will do 'im a power o' good."

How was he to resist? Dick came up from Oxford so seldom. Besides, Dick knew that he might have dined at Hadscombe. How could he refuse to go out? Looking over Mrs. Clutterbuck's shoulder, Gaskony saw *The Athenian* filing-cabinets opened to receive him, and he said to himself: I won't go. I'll stay and do my own job; but Mrs. Clutterbuck said:

"I laid out your evening clothes, Sir William—studs and links an' all. . . ." Then, seeing his face, she added coaxingly: "I should go if I was you. Mr. Dick, 'e'd be that disappointed! Besides, there's other evenings as you'll be alone, like it or not."

Gaskony went into his bedroom to dress and, when he was dressed, into the living-room. Still Dick had not come, and Gaskony opened the glass-paned doors of what he called his "private" book-case. From it he took down the volume of *Marius the Epicurean* which had been in Julia's hands when his eyes had first fallen upon her in the Chancery Lane shop forty-two years ago. To-day was her birthday and, thinking only of her young face—the deep lower lip, the wide uplooking eyes whose dark gaze had fallen upon him like a cool breeze upon warm flesh that shudders and glows—he opened and began to read:

> . . . in the streets of Pisa. And as oftenest happens also, with natures of genuinely poetic quality, those piecemeal beginnings came suddenly to harmonious completeness among the fortunate incidents, the physical heat and light, of one singularly happy day.
>
> It was one of the first hot days of March—"the sacred day"—on which, from Pisa, as from many another harbour in the Mediterranean, the *Ship of Isis* went to sea, and everyone walked down to the shore-side to witness the freighting of the vessel, its launching and final abandonment among the waves, as an object really devoted to the Great Goddess, that new rival, or "double", of ancient Venus, and like her a favourite patroness of sailors. On the evening next before, all the world had been abroad to view the illumination of the river; the stately lines of building being wreathed with hundreds of many-coloured lamps. The young men had poured forth their chorus—
>
> > "Cras amet qui nunquam amavit
> > Quique amavit cras amet"—

as they bore their torches through the yielding crowd, or rowed their lanterned boats up and down the stream, till far into the night, when heavy rain-drops had driven the last lingerers home. Morning broke, however—

Dick was standing in the doorway, his face alight with pleasure and the satisfaction of giving pleasure. No sooner had he been offered sherry than he produced the theatre-tickets proudly from his waistcoat-pocket: the fourth row of the stalls, next the centre-gangway; and Gaskony knew that Dick, in ancient dinner-jacket and rumpled shirt, his curly yellow hair, as yet scarcely touched by white, pluming up from a sun-tanned fore-head, was feeling young to-night, had put away the respon-sibility of his College, and, in his capacity of man-of-the-world, was bent upon giving his brother a treat. Gaskony responded to his mood—no longer the Judge or "old Gasky", but Will, who had always been supposed to know his way about less well than Dick and who, in the ordering of meals, the choosing of pleasures and the making of journeys was expected to yield to Dick's leadership. Dick was "executive", Will was not; that was the understanding between them. How odd that an Oxford don should suppose that he knew more of the world than a judge! But this delusion of Dick's was one that Will Gaskony never challenged. In all their expeditions, Dick chose everything, paid for everything, and at the end, after a pause for mental arithmetic, apportioned their shares of the cost.

Now he had chosen the play and, by one of those miracles which were always at his command, had secured at the last moment the best seats in the house. He was about to explain how this miracle had been accomplished when he noticed the volume in his brother's hand and took it abruptly.

"*Marius*," he said. "How's your *Athenian*?"

Will spread out his hands, then quickly took *Marius* away and returned it to its shelf. They talked of the play they were going to see, of Oxford, of the possibility of their taking a holiday together in the Long Vacation. They spread a map of

France on the carpet and kneeled beside it until the clock struck eight.

"Eight!" said Dick. "There's not a hope of dinner if we're to be in time for the curtain."

"Your responsibility," Will answered. "You're in charge of parties."

"In that case," Dick said, "the revised plan is this. Bread and cheese here, now, and a pint of champagne. Eight-twenty, taxi. After the play, supper at Rodd's."

6

AFTER supper, a good, leisurely supper that warmed the heart, they went upstairs to the Egg Room at Rodd's. Its fireplace curves into the narrow end of the egg; from its bow-window, in the broad end, you may look down to St. James's Palace or up to Boodle's rival bow; and its fluted ceiling is claimed by architectural members to be one of the Seven Graces of Europe. On entering the room, you glance at the ceiling politely, as seamen, in boarding a warship, salute the quarter-deck, and Dick Gaskony, on his way to the bow-window, performed the admiring rite.

"All the same," he said, drawing back the curtains and looking across the lighted road at Berry's, "important though it is to have a roof over your head, it is equally important to have a great wine-merchant at your feet. What should we do if we were cut off from France? . . . You know, Will, it has always puzzled me that your Athenians produced so great a civilization on such poor wine. And I doubt whether even the Romans—your Marius or Horace himself—had much palate as we understand it. I distrust that Salernian four years old . . ." This was intended to lead the conversation gently to the subject that was on Dick's mind, but the transition did not come as easily as he had hoped. In the end, he plunged:

"Why won't you talk about your *Athenian*, Will? You used to—with me?"

"Who says I won't talk of it?"

"Anyhow you don't. Are you stuck? I mean, can I help?"

"No, Dick," the Judge answered with a little jerk of his head sideways—the jerk of a shying horse. "There's no particular

[31]

snag. I'm not stuck because—well, because, to tell you the truth, I haven't really begun—the writing, I mean."

"But why not? The material's complete?"

"I suppose so. Yes—so far as material for a book of that kind can ever be said to be complete."

"Then why in heaven's name don't you get down to it?"

The Judge was silent, and his brother with affectionate persuasions encouraged and goaded him, saying that he had now been retired from the Bench two whole years; that the great book, which he alone was equipped to write, lay open, waiting to be written; that if he did not begin now, he might never see the end.

"I know," Dick said, "that, if the book were mine, I could die happy, having written it. The fame it would bring—not a cheap popularity, but a lovely, enduring honour—would keep me warm in my old age."

"But it's not that I want," the Judge exclaimed. "I'm completely without ambition—always have been. Fame—enduring honour—oh, I'm not being damned superior; I don't in the least despise them or undervalue them. They're legitimate incentives, just rewards. But it happens that I have no one to share them with, and so——"

"All right," Dick interrupted. "So be it. Cut out the fame and honour. Cut out the rewards. Still, the thing itself—simply to have written such a book, isn't that——"

"No," the Judge put in with sudden emphasis. "Not to *have* written it. Not the result, the effect. Not even, perhaps, to *write* it. But to think it, to live and be in it—that's what I hanker after. The glory I want is—" and he looked nervously at his brother before entrusting him with this inmost confidence—"is, if you'll let the phrase pass, the, the glory of that excluding thought. You see, Dick, the subject of the book is more than Periclean Athens—more than the conditions, the way of life, the political and moral ideas prevailing there at that time. The subject is also the *feel* of being alive then, and the feel of being alive at any time depends, for a sensitive man, on the tug of the past and the tug of the future. In a sense, he's connected by live

[32]

wires—through heredity, through vision, through his aware-
ness of the eternal gods—with other thought in other times.
Only a fool thinks of himself as a Modern with a capital M.
No one is ever at the head of Time's procession. The past
catches at his coat-tails sometimes, and sometimes jostles and
shoves him on; and sometimes the future drags him forward
with unseen hands, and sometimes, when he's least expecting it,
pushes him back—as we push back a kitten that's over-eager for
a dish of milk. . . . And so, you see," the Judge added, "really
my subject isn't just Periclean Athens but the timelessness, the
wonderful interdependence, of experience as it was *felt* in
Periclean Athens. That sense of timelessness underlies all experience, but it was felt differently then and now. The
Athenians were less burdened by the past than we are. They
were younger; the directness of their literature says so. I think
they were also less afraid of the future because they were less
conscious of it. . . . And so what I have to do is not chiefly to
write and produce A Book, but to plunge deeper and deeper
into *my* experience until mine and the Athenian's—d'you see
what I'm getting at?—until he and I meet at a level far below
the superficiality of our distinct historical periods, until——"

"Until," said Dick Gaskony with a grin, "you and he *click*
in a timeless common humanity? Is that it?" He leaned forward
and patted his brother's knee. "You and I—and Phil Brown—
used to talk like this when we were very young. Thank the
Lord we're still capable of it! You know, Will, you are the
oddest mixture of an undergraduate and an old fogey. You sit
about in London inventing reasons—all of them good reasons—
for not doing the real work of your life. You aren't practical
enough, or ruthless enough, or self-confident enough to be true
to yourself and——"

"That's the second time to-day I've been told I'm not being
true to myself," the Judge said. "Oh, Dick, I know! I don't
really need telling!"

"Who else told you?"

"Vivien.

"A woman," Dick said. He rose, walked across the room and

[33]

rang the bell. There was a long silence between the brothers
while the waiter came and drinks were ordered and brought.
Then, laying down an illustrated paper in which he had meanwhile buried himself, Dick added: "So Vivien told you that, did
she? I wonder what would have happened if you had married,
Will. A woman, who understood what you were driving at,
wouldn't have let you nibble your life away. If you had
married——"

"That was impossible," the Judge said.

"Impossible? Why?"

"Because, as you well know, Dick, she wouldn't have me."

"That," Dick answered, "was many years ago."

"You mean, I should have married some other woman? That's
because even you don't know the whole story. You came into
it after Phil Brown and I knew Julia. You don't know the
beginning and you don't really know the end. You don't know
why—so I thought—she and I belonged to each other or why,
when it was Phil she married, it seemed to me—oh no, not
bitter, not even precisely a disappointment, but untrue, unreal,
as if it hadn't happened, as if she were still mine, as if— Do you
know why I was reading *Marius* this evening when you came
in? It's her birthday to-day, and she had that book—I mean
that particular volume—in her hands when I first saw her.
That's the bit you don't know."

He leaned back and for a moment shut his eyes. Opening
them again, he continued: "It was my first year at the Bar. I
was briefless; there were expenses in chambers, debts, too,
incurred in getting called to the Bar; I was utterly poor. Phil
was poor enough too, but he had a tiny allowance from his
father, and he earned a few guineas now and then in Fleet
Street. He kept our lodging together when I had nothing, and
when I got a bit of tutoring I paid him back shilling by shilling.
Anyhow, it was damned close—hungry as often as not—and
one day, walking down Chancery Lane, I saw the two volumes
of *Marius* in a window, second-hand. They wanted eight
and sixpence. I hadn't got it, but I cut down food by three-
pence a day and calculated that I should have my *Marius* in

five weeks. I asked the bookseller to keep it for me. He said he'd try but he couldn't promise, and every morning and every evening I looked to see if it was still in the window. One day it vanished—but only from the window; it was still in the shop; and that time the bookseller, seeing that the book was the Holy Grail to me, *did* promise to keep it until the end of the five weeks. No good. One night I had a fever: I had to buy quinine. Then the side of one of my boots split and it had to be patched. That put me out of my stride, and I was shy, I felt I hadn't kept my contract, I didn't want the bookseller to guess that I—Mr. William Gaskony, of the Middle Temple, Barrister-at-Law—was poor right down to pennies and a patch on my boots. So I didn't dare to ask him to keep *Marius* any longer. I didn't dare even to go in to see if it was still there. And in the end, when I had the money, I went into the shop with the coins, not in my pocket, but all hot, clutched in my hand—like a boy buying sweets. 'I've come,' I said, 'for *Marius the Epicurean.*'"

Will Gaskony shrugged his shoulders and stretched out a hand for his glass. "Of course—it would be so," he continued, "—you can guess that I was too late. The story wouldn't be a story if I hadn't been. The bookseller cocked an eyebrow and jerked a thumb and said: 'That lady's just bought it and now she's choosing more.' I stared; she had the volume in her hands, reading it; and, as I stared, her eyes came up to me." At this the Judge paused and looked at his brother, and said, as though there were nothing more on earth that needed saying: "At that time she was twenty-two years old." Then he added: "I suppose she saw that something was up. She said: 'What is it?'—not to me but to the bookseller—and she let the book close with her finger in it to mark the place. The bookseller explained, I think, how I had been after the book for near seven weeks, but what he said I don't know; I wasn't listening to him, but looking at her—and she at last to me. 'Well,' she said, 'of course it's yours,' and handed it to me, open at the place. I noticed—it was as quick as that—that her hand . . . I noticed," the Judge continued, struggling to convey the impossibly contradictory truth, "that on her hand (which didn't seem to be, at the instant, *her* hand at all) was a wedding-ring. There must have been a bit of me, I suppose, that saw it as a disaster; otherwise I shouldn't have noticed it at all; but all the same, it was irrelevant; it didn't in the least affect what I had seen and was seeing. I took the book and held it, still open as she gave it to me. She must have asked why it was important to me, for I found myself saying what I had never said before —not to you, not even to Phil at that time—that I was going to write a book about the Greeks and that *Marius* was . . . Anyhow, in three minutes I must have pretty thoroughly poured my heart out. She took it as the most natural thing in the world; just accepted my Great Work calmly and glowingly, as if she'd been in at the planning of it in a previous existence or had read it in a later one. 'You ought to meet my husband,' she said. 'He's a Greek scholar. He's an invalid.' I handed over my coins and we went out of the shop together. At home, when I got there, I still had a finger in the place at which she had been reading and I sat down on the table-edge and read, looking for an omen. It was the bit about the Ship of Isis. . . . 'And as oftenest happens also,' I read, 'with natures of genuinely poetic quality, those piecemeal beginnings came suddenly to harmonious completeness among the fortunate incidents, the physical heat and light, of one singularly happy day.'"

At this point, another member, unknown to the two brothers, had come into the room, and was hovering over the table on which the illustrated papers lay. Will Gaskony checked his narrative and looked at the fluted ceiling.

7

THE plain structure of the tale Dick already knew well enough. Julia, the daughter of Edward Springster, a civil engineer in private practice in Westminster, had married two years earlier one of his assistants, named Pellagrin, who had turned from the classics after leaving Cambridge and swung his whole talent into engineering, not, as might have been supposed, for practical, money-making reasons, but with a prophet's zeal. Engineering had appeared to him as an emblem of progress, a guarantee against what he, the son of a schoolmaster, had most feared in himself: polite enslavement to the classical grind. Julia had shared his idealism, and their marriage, lighted by it, had been happy, hard-working, devotedly at ease; but early in its second year Roy Pellagrin had been struck down by paralysis which, though he survived it, in effect ended his life. The year Ninety-Two, in which, after the bookshop encounter, Will Gaskony and Phil Brown began to become almost a part of the Pellagrins' household had been of all its years the darkest. Misfortune had declared itself but neither Roy nor Julia was adjusted to it; they still dreamed of a complete recovery and were entangled in false hopes. As hope faded, they became, in a sense, happier, their once eager love changing to love different in kind, and the enthusiasm, which they had once shared, to a modest, accepting compassion. When Dick Gaskony had first been introduced by his brother into the little circle, he had been aware of no tension within it except of that created by what was indeed unmistakable—the invalid's willingness to die, a willingness the more impressive because there was neither despair nor self-pity in it, only what Julia called

"Roy's burnt-outness", his not desiring or clamouring or cling-ing. She, for her part, made no pretence that his old ardour could be, or ought to be, re-illumined; she was loyal to the changed conditions of their life, not to an irrecoverable past; and it was, perhaps, this loyalty of hers which had hidden from Dick, for several years, that both his brother and Phil Brown were in love with her and had withheld them from perceiving it in each other. How soon or how late the truth dawned upon them and upon her, Dick didn't know, and, when the member who had strolled into the Egg Room had strolled out again, he said to his brother:

"That was a queer party, you two, and Julia, and Pellagrin in his wheeled-chair. More than a dozen years of it before he died, and all of you as blind as bats! Or weren't you?"

"She can't have been," the Judge answered. "There must have been a kind of tacit knowledge between her and Phil, though I'll swear they never spoke of it while Roy lived. You see," he added, "the world has flowed on since then. And, even by the standards of that time, Phil and I were old-fashioned. We didn't, to put it simply, make love to married women, and, what's more, a married woman who cared for her husband as Julia did for hers wasn't open to it. I loved her, but I didn't say so, even to myself. I called it friendship. So it was. I haven't a doubt that Phil did likewise. When we talked of her, we talked on that basis. I hadn't the least sense of con-cealing anything from him, nor he, I suppose, of concealing anything from me. The best proof is that for years none of us used Christian names—she was 'Mrs. Pellagrin' even in our own talk—and when we did come to Christian names we did so *together*, at her suggestion, in her husband's presence—a con-ventional lifting of the convention, a formal pact. It wasn't so much because we obeyed the rules as because, even inside ourselves, we didn't question them, that we were what you call 'blind'. Seems odd now, looking back. My friendship with her was so intimate through all the time in which I was climbing at the Bar that it didn't occur to me that her friendship with anyone else, with Phil Brown in particular, could be more intimate. And I don't believe it was. When her husband died at the end of Nineteen-Four, I was pretty prosperous—anyhow in a position to marry, and poor Phil wasn't. He'd stuck to his writing; none of the fleshpots for him; apart from one novel that sold a bit, nothing went further than was necessary to keep the wolf from the door. That he might marry didn't strike me. I made no sort of haste. Anyhow the conventions held, Pellagrin being not long in his grave; and I remember, in the Long Vacation of Nineteen-Five, Julia and I used to go for great walks in the country together; we'd spend the whole day in the open and come back to dine in London, Phil joining us as often as not, and I assumed—" Will Gaskony broke off and looked at his brother with a wry smile for his own folly. "I assumed that we were, in effect, betrothed, without words because there was no need of them. . . . Oh yes, I did, God help me for a fool! I assumed that, in not speaking, not hurrying and pressing, I was doing what she wished, and that when 'after a decent interval' I did speak, we should—how shall I put it?—ratify our treaty, not make it. I was hopelessly wrong simply because I was, up to a point, so deeply right. She did love me, and it was that which prevented me from grasping that she loved Phil in a more—anyhow, that she loved him differently. Even so, if Phil and I had still been in lodgings together as we were in the old days, I suppose I should have scented what was in the air. As it was, I didn't. I thought she was mine. It sounds like arrogance and vanity. It wasn't. It seemed like knowledge, shared between her and me."

The Judge rose from his chair and stood, with one knee on the window-seat, his back to the room, looking out at the night sky.

"That's why I haven't married another woman," he said. "Inside me, it was already done. Her marriage to Phil didn't affect it. Or her death when Vivien was born. Or his death. Nothing. I think of Vivien as my child—hers and mine. Do you understand that?"

"No," Dick said. "I understand it of *you*—that it's true of you. But I don't imaginatively apply it to myself. It seems——"

"Sentimental?"

"No, not in the least. On the contrary—impossibly stoical."

"Ah!" the Judge exclaimed. "Then you understand it all right. Just leave out the 'impossibly'."

One of their long brotherly silences fell. Dick, filling and lighting his second pipe, looked at the long, straight back. "You were always a window-gazer, Will. Come back out of it, and tell me——"

"At any rate," the Judge cut in, "you can understand why I value that book more than anything in the world." He turned from the window towards his chair, and there, beyond the table, smiling and rubbing his hands, was Severidge.

"What book?" he asked.

At first neither of the brothers answered. Dick supposed that Will would speak, but a glance at Will's face, the eyes wide, the lips compressed, a contorted mask-like face, showed him that from that quarter no answer would come, and he said: "We were speaking of *Marius*."

The tone was discouraging, but Severidge had dined well, had driven his guests home, was exhilarated by what he called car-exercise, and was proof against discouragement. He swung round a chair and joined them.

"That's extraordinarily interesting," he said, and might, perhaps, have said more if the Judge, coming out of his trance, had not observed with a kind of sepulchral politeness: "*Marius the Epicurean*, you know," evidently unaware of the gap in time between the asking of Severidge's question and his answering it.

Severidge laughed—a light, good-humoured laugh which, whether or not it was so intended, had the effect of covering the Judge's awkwardness, and plunged, with the oddest mixture of genuine interest and sharp, persistent curiosity, into a monologue on Walter Pater, full of knowledge and of what passed for modesty, though empty of sensibility. Now I understand for the first time, Dick Gaskony thought, why that little man is said to be attractive to women. The curiosity, which infuriates poor Will, is for them "interest" or "sympathy".

Severidge is interested in their clothes, their ambitions, their love-affairs, their whole psychological "set-up", as he is in Will's *Marius*, and what Will shrinks from they respond to. That is the man's secret. He doesn't look through women; he looks at them. He remembers everything, I'll be bound—what they said, what they wore three years ago—and forgets only that it was three years ago. He is never bored, never impersonal, never doubtful; always curious, possessive, confident—"you leave it to me, my dear, put it out of your mind, trouble no more about it; I am a magician because I am interested, because I understand you personally, because the luck of the world goes with me, and all difficulties bow down when I pass, like a row of waiters and bell-boys as I enter a hotel!" That, thought Dick Gaskony, watching Severidge's keen, complacent, smiling face, is the key that opens doors for him, and makes women, even highly intelligent women, say that he is charming; and yet it is by no means the key to— From Severidge's face he looked to his brother's and what he saw there shocked him out of the cool, amused analysis with which, at Severidge's expense, he had been lightly entertaining himself. He had supposed that Will had been annoyed by the intrusion—disproportionately annoyed, perhaps; but it was not annoyance that he saw now in his brother's eyes but an emotion that he had never before seen in them—fear? rage?—an indescribable cold passion as of a threatened army drawing back into its fortress, as of an assaulted animal defiantly terror-stricken within its den. Will was not frowning as he frowned in common wrath. His eyebrows were up, his eyes deeply and fixedly gazing; below them two sharply-defined areas of pallor had risen on his cheeks. Severidge, seeming unaware, talked and bantered.

"Come, Gaskony, what's the mystery? Why is this book so damned precious?" He turned to Dick. "I didn't know he had anything to conceal." Then, persistently, back to the Judge, blindly throwing pebbles of jocularity at the old animal in its den. "Come. You can't leave *that* story unfinished! You may as well make a clean breast of it!"

"Why?" said the Judge.

"Why? Because——"

"Well," said the Judge, drawing back into his chair and lowering his head, "since you insist, since you insist, I'll tell you why. I value that book because it was given me by the woman who might have been my wife. Her hands touched it. . . . And now for God's sake leave me alone."

Severidge was profuse in his apologies. He had overheard, he said, a remark which to him, as a connoisseur of books, had naturally been interesting. He had had no idea that he was interrupting a private conversation of—well, of that degree of privacy. He was afraid he had been tactless and foolish. He could say only that he was sorry, that it had been far from his wish to——

"Oh, say no more of it," the Judge said. "I spoke too sharply. I let my feelings get the better of me."

"Then we part friends, I hope?"

"Certainly. Certainly."

When Severidge was gone, Dick Gaskony said: "Let's have another drink, Will, before we go home We'll walk. It's a clear night."

And Will Gaskony answered: "Sorry, Dick. . . . Made a fool of myself. . . . Excessive. . . . Worst of it is I shall have to be devilish affable to him when next we meet, and he to me."

Severidge, driving himself home to South Street, was putting two and two together. His memory brought forward his knowledge that Vivien Lerrick's mother had first been met by the Judge in a bookshop in Chancery Lane, and he laid this fact beside what he had just been told of *Marius*. Any link? He'd find out on Tuesday when young Lerrick and his wife came to dinner. . . . He slid the car neatly into its garage. . . . I wonder what the old boy would, in fact, take for that book? Not that I or anyone else wants it. But still—it's a part of himself; ridiculous though it may seem, it *is* himself; to sell it would be, for him, to sell himself. What *would* he take? . . . While he was undressing, the question recurred to Severidge, and he said to his mirror: You damned fool. What the hell do you want with his *Marius*? Why can't you leave the poor chap alone?

. . . In bed, he remembered the old lady in Scotland and her Cennini manuscript. Probably her treasure. Inherited, certainly. She didn't sound like a collector. The Cennini was her pride. . . . At that moment, no doubt, she was asleep in her little house. He switched on his bed-light and sat up, as though to look at her, and reached for a cigarette; but discipline refused the cigarette. He must sleep six hours. He lay down and slept instantly.

8

WHILE the two brothers were at Rodd's, Vivien and Henry Lerrick had passed through one of those periods of tension, passionate, childish and desperate, which were frequent in their lives. As soon as Henry returned from seeing off the Judge, he had gone into the small library, avoiding encounter with her. When she reminded him that he must get up the wine and dress for dinner, he had obeyed wearily and looked at her, as he passed, from the depths of some far-distant agitation. In the company of his guests he had recovered, or seemed to recover, his good spirits, but she had known that this required courage of him. When the guests were gone, he maintained his gaiety, gave her more drink, turned on the gramophone, danced with her alone. They went upstairs laughing, and stood together at the open window of their bedroom, smelling the garden scents.

Afterwards, neither slept. Vivien sat up in bed and said: "We aren't sleeping, Henry. Shall I turn on the light?" He said: "Yes, darling, turn on the light," and rose, put on his dressing-gown and took a cigarette from the china box on the mantelpiece. She began to tell him without preface, as though she were continuing a discussion, what Gasky had said about their putting the house on the market—that, as long as they kept the price at seventeen thousand pounds, it wasn't really on the market at all.

"That's true," Henry said.

"Then why——?"

"We'll reduce the price to-morrow. We'll make it ten thousand. . . . Eight if you like. . . . We've got to sell, Vivien. We've got to get out."

"Where to?" she asked.

"I don't know yet. A boarding-house. Anywhere. But we must stop the leak."

"All right," she said. "I agree." Then, after a momentary pause: "How bad is it? You had better tell me."

He seated himself on the bed and told her about the Waynford Trust. He was solicitor to the Trust. Two mortgages had been repaid to the trustees. Money had come in, too, from other sources. The trust-deed allowed a certain freedom of reinvestment, and the trustees had decided to keep the money in the bank until they had made up their minds and a good opportunity occurred. Meanwhile, he had had control of the money.

"I borrowed it," he said.

"Borrowed?"

"Only for a few hours. Forty-eight hours, I thought."

He had had inside knowledge that a merger between Maxite Asbestos and Consolidated Asbestos Properties was about to be announced. Maxite was a small company. Its shares, which had once touched thirty shillings, were at eight. On the merger they would have jumped to fourteen or more. He had bought a long line of them.

"How many?" Vivien asked.

"Forty thousand. I looked for a profit of thirteen—ten at least."

"Forty," Vivien repeated. "I can't do the sum. What did they cost?"

"Sixteen thousand pounds odd."

"And now?"

"Sixpence nominal."

"That means—nothing?" His silence acknowledged it. "Then," she said, "what we owe is sixteen thousand pounds. If we sold the house, that would still leave eight."

He hesitated. Faced by her calm willingness to accept the truth, he had an almost invincible tendency to lighten it, but he brought himself to tell her that the sale of the house would by no means yield eight. She had forgotten that it was mortgaged. Its sale at eight thousand would yield them a clear two; its contents perhaps another two.

She nodded: "That leaves us owing twelve—and loose debts? Would thirteen clear us?"

Again he hesitated, then got up from the bed and walked away to the curtained window. Further than this, as yet, he could not bring himself to go. It hadn't occurred to her to ask why he had been driven to seek a gambler's profit in Maxite. What she called "loose debts" had already amounted, not to one, but to over three thousand pounds; his own bank was pressing for this. His mother had, moreover, inherited from his father an obligation, in her own name, to Bright's heirs. This, in capital and accumulated interest, stood now at nearly seven thousand, and Henry had guaranteed it. Three and seven made ten. Add the Waynford sixteen: twenty-six. Of this, three could stand over; if Bright's heirs were given four, they wouldn't press for the balance. Twenty-three were urgent.

All he said was: "No use counting on a sale, Vivien. It will take time. Meanwhile——"

"How hard are the Waynford people pressing?" she asked.

"They aren't as yet. Humphrey Waynford still thinks the money's safe in the bank. But he came to see me this morning to discuss reinvestment. Next week we are both to have a conference with his broker. If they decide to buy, I have to produce cash and you see——"

"Henry," she said, "this—this isn't just bankruptcy? I mean——"

"Yes," he answered, "it's criminal all right. It's odd. It doesn't feel like it. . . . I wasn't stealing the Waynford money. Of course, I knew Maxite *might* fall. Even so, I meant to sell quick and somehow find the difference. Then they fell a shilling. I held because my information was that the merger was still on. Then they fell another two—and nearly half the money was gone."

She asked him why he had gambled *so much*—why sixteen thousand pounds? The answer was that he had already needed seven urgently—ten to be clear; but still he could not bring himself to give this answer, and he gave no answer at all. She held out her hand so that he had to come forward and take it. She made him sit again on the side of the bed and put her arms round him.

"I suppose we have been fools," she said. "We have been spending too much. . . . Henry!"

"What, my dear?"

"When we have come through this, we shan't do it again? We shan't be like the people who go on and on?"

"You talk," he said, "as if it were your fault too. . . . No, Vivien, I shan't go on and on. I'm not naturally any kind of waster. But you know, Bright, Lerrick was in a bit of a mess when I took over. My mother owed money to Bright's heirs. That's what set me back." To say this comforted him. It was almost as if he had told the truth that he had concealed from her. His mind ranged forward to next week's meeting with Humphrey Waynford and his stockbroker. They would sit round a table discussing how to invest money that didn't exist. Afterwards, Humphrey was to lunch with him at Rodd's. Should he make a clean breast of it? Humphrey was an easy-going chap who wouldn't want—but, easy-going or not, Humphrey was a trustee; he couldn't shut his eyes to a criminal conversion of Trust funds. . . .

"To-morrow," Vivien said, "we shall see it more clearly. It's no good letting the thing go round and round in our heads. Let's sleep if we can."

They lay down and turned out the light.

On Saturdays, Bright, Lerrick did not open their office, and Henry, on the terrace after breakfast, in the sunshine that might have been the grace of a holiday, itched for action—for some device or plan, some miracle, that should save him. The week-end appeared to him as his opportunity, perhaps the last. What could he do? Borrow again? But who would lend him twenty-three, or even sixteen, thousand pounds? Could he raise it in smaller packets if he took the car from the garage now and journeyed from friend to friend? His heart turned against this piecemeal begging; it might defer the evil but would not end it; and he desired to prove to himself and to Vivien that he was not one of those who "go on and on"; he wanted to shoulder his responsibility and work for his salvation.

For the same reason, he had put aside Vivien's suggestion that he should go to the Judge. He knew well enough that Gasky lived on his pension and the income from a small capital; he couldn't, if he wanted to, write a cheque for twenty-three thousand or anything approaching it; all he could give was advice. "I want his advice," Vivien had said, "it would help to talk it over with him"; but Henry had persuaded her to wait. "If there's a way out of this," he said, "I should like to find it without calling on him. Let's leave him out of it, at any rate until after Tuesday night." Vivien had said: "Why Tuesday night?" and he had answered: "I don't know. No reason in particular, but let's leave it until then."

He had said "Tuesday" because it had been in his mind that they were to dine with Severidge that evening, and because he had had what he considered a reasonable long-term hope of getting work from C.M.I. One thing leads to another, Henry had thought when he was invited to South Street, and he had determined not to let the grass grow under his feet. Now, on the terrace, pressing out a cigarette in the saucer of his coffee cup, he perceived that long-term hopes from C.M.I. did not match the urgency of his present need. Tuesday evening was irrelevant. Why had he said "Tuesday evening"? He supposed that every defaulting solicitor from the beginning of time had clung to straws, and had believed, until the last moment, that some miracle would save him.

In the midst of this hopelessness the telephone rang, and his heart bounded with nameless hope. Perhaps this was his chance; perhaps, when he came back from the telephone, his way would lie open. But the voice was Humphrey Waynford's. He wanted to fix the day on which they were to go into the City next week, and Henry could do no more than postpone it until Thursday.

Having put down the receiver, he said to himself: At least, there's one honest, practical thing I can do, and he drove into Croydon, reduced the price of the house to "ten thousand or offer" and had a preliminary discussion with the auctioneer about the sale of the contents. Then, at home, he rang for Kingsley, and told her that a man would be coming to make a catalogue. "And people may come with orders to view the house. Perhaps you will tell the others, Kingsley. There's no hurry. But you ought to be looking for another place."

"It seems a pity," Kingsley said. "I remember you here, sir, coming home from Cambridge, and theatricals on the lawn."

"It is a pity," Henry said. "But we can't afford it, Kingsley. That's the plain fact."

"Well, I'm sorry, I'm sure, sir. The Judge, he'll be sorry too. But there it is. Facts are facts as you might say, and it's not everyone nowadays has the sense to take them by the forelock."

9

SEVERIDGE came home early on Tuesday evening and bathed and dressed at leisure. Nothing pleased him more than the breaks in routine which he sometimes allowed himself. Suddenly, without explanation, he had cancelled two engagements, leaving his staff at C.M.I. to say what they chose. "I am going home," he had said, and gone.

When he was dressed, there was still half an hour before the Lerricks' coming, and he went out on to the balcony of his drawing-room from which steps led down to a lawn. The shadow of masonry darkened a triangle of the lawn, making the greater part of it, lighted by the sun, appear the more brilliantly green, and Severidge regarded this precious space, a gleaming evidence of his own wealth and of his gardeners' care, with more satisfaction than any country garden could have afforded him. In his hand was a large, pale-gold Martini. A sip told him that some fool—the young footman, presumably —had put too much vermouth into it. He returned to the drawing-room and mixed an Old Fashioned for himself. Even in the United States it had been a long time before he had encountered an Old Fashioned in its perfection. Everything depended, of course, on your having *old* Bourbon whiskey . . . half a lump, not a whole lump, of sugar at the bottom of the glass; *no* angostura—not even three drops as the heathen supposed; then Bourbon; fill up with ice, and float a slice of orange on top—float it, not squeeze it. He added a cherry for its rosy colour and went out on to the balcony again. Perfect. He watched the fountain, on the lawn below him, cast up its plume into the evening light.

10

Henry and Vivien's drive from Hadscombe into London for their dinner with Severidge was a series of short sharp outbursts of conversation divided by iron silences. Vivien glanced at Henry in fear that he might fall asleep at the wheel.

"Poor Henry, you're worn out."

"Worn out with doing nothing," he said. "No, my dear, I'm all right. Don't add me to your worries," and he pressed down the accelerator.

Silence. The brazen clangour of a passing tram. She looked at Henry's profile—the head lifted, the abrupt chin out-thrust —and at the curve of his wrist from which the glove was furled back, and remembered the happiness of being driven by him when they had been happy. She felt now that they would never be at ease with each other again. She longed to cry, to find refuge, to wake from nightmare, but she interlaced her fingers tightly and kept a hold upon herself. Her mind was overflowing with a clear, unswerving acknowledgment of what Henry had done, a recognition of its guilt and folly, and a sense as clear, as unswerving, that whatever Henry Lerrick, the solicitor, had done, the man within him, whom she knew and loved, was not contemptible, not to be deserted. She bit her lip, dry-eyed.

The week-end had been fruitless. They had argued until they were exhausted. They had even flamed at each other—or at the blank futility of their discussions. They had said the words which, they knew, must have been spoken by thousands of others before. He had said: "The horrible thing is I've done this to you. What is to become of you?" She had said: "Try

117627

not to worry about me, Henry. I shall be all right." Everything
they had said, even their words of love and reassurance, had
seemed mechanical and useless. Long silences had fallen. At
night, they had lain awake in silence, side by side. An element
of falseness had seemed to enter even into the grasp of a hand.
Now, in the car, they were silent again.

At last Henry said: "Vivien!"

"Henry."

"We've got to get through this evening."

"I know."

"I've got a kind of hunch that this introduction to C.M.I.
might lead——"

"O my dear one!"

"I know," he said with a glance towards her, "my hunches
don't seem very reliable. Still——"

"I didn't mean that."

"Never mind. You had a right to. . . . The real point is
that—just as a matter of—well, of not chucking our hands in,
we've got to put on an act. You're the intelligent one. You get
Severidge on to *ideas*. He likes that."

"And you?"

"Oh, I shall be cheerful and inquiring."

11

When the Lerricks came, Severidge was delighted to see them. They would reflect his glow.

"So you are Vivien!" he said. "Does my old friendship with the Judge entitle me to call you that? Now, sit down both of you, and, while you contemplate the fountain, decide what cocktail you will have."

He had no other guests that evening except his elder sister, Mrs. Sarrett, and when she appeared, small, correct and squirrel-like, Vivien supposed at first that she was a secretary, so little did Severidge take account of her. Gradually her character emerged as that of a permitted ironist. She irritated her brother but he liked her to pull his leg.

"I have been telling Lerrick," he explained, "that this evening I stopped the clock for them."

"Ah!" she said, obediently taking her cue but investing her obedience with a quality of her own, "that is extremely important. You don't know, Mrs. Lerrick, how great a compliment that is. What George calls 'stopping the clock' is what Americans mean by 'relaxing'. It doesn't mean just being casually lazy like the rest of us; it means being actively inactive. You lie down flat on your back and think of each limb in turn— of how lazy it's being. Then you have a bath, and dress much more slowly than usual, and you sit down somewhere—on this balcony perhaps—and think hard of the engagements you would have been keeping if you hadn't cancelled them; and then you think *forward* to the pleasure that's coming, whatever it is: in this case, to the arrival of very special guests. Isn't that right, George?"

"That's right enough," Severidge answered, "but you make it sound a terrible rigmarole, Molly. They will think I'm some kind of new-thought crank. Really it's quite simple," he continued, turning to Vivien. "We busy men are always in danger of allowing the clock to get us down. However much we delegate, however determined we may be to concern ourselves only with the essentials of policy, detail gradually grows upon us; every minute of every day becomes occupied; routine begins to wind its tentacles around us; little by little we lose our freedom—we become slaves: the slaves of those who depend upon us—the managers, the assistant managers, the slaves even of our secretaries and our manservants: all of them expect us to do such and such a thing at such and such a time. Then we begin to expect ourselves to do such and such a thing at such and such a time; we become slaves of ourselves; we take a petty mechanical pride in our invariableness; we think of our regularity as something heroic and splendid as though it were the regularity of the planets, and forget that it is only the regularity of a little slavish clock that our secretary winds up every morning. And so, you see, now and then I stop the clock. I have no regular holiday; I don't play golf; week-ends aren't sacred to me; I have no routine-leisure of any kind, except a fixed minimum of sleep. Routine-leisure is no good because that, too, is clock-bound. No man is anything but a slave who isn't capable, like Napoleon, of stopping in the middle of a battle to sleep for half an hour, or who can't suddenly scrap all his engagements and go off to the Aegean, or who doesn't say to himself sometimes: This is Tuesday evening. I have charming guests. I'm going to enjoy myself. I've done enough work for to-day. Stop the clock!"

He paused and smiled at Vivien as if to say: That performance was given for you; but it was to Henry that he addressed a final question: "Now, Lerrick, how does that strike you? To you, as a busy professional man, does it seem to make sense?"

"It seems to me," said Henry, "first-rate for Napoleon and the chairman of C.M.I."

"Good, good!" Severidge exclaimed. "Yes, it's true, I suppose, that you can't in the same way cancel appointments with your clients. Still, the principle holds?"

"Well, yes," Henry replied. "And so would the practice if Vivien and I had a yacht that would take us to the Aegean."

Severidge laughed his approval of this good-humoured young man. "So you have, so you have!" he said. "Next time I go, will you come with me?" He spoke this to Vivien, but added without pause: "Both of you? Good. Is that a bet? Now let us go in and have a little dinner. I thought, as the weather was warm, we would begin with a glass of Montrachet."

As they moved in from the balcony, Henry was able to say to his wife: "How he loves to say his piece! Do you think we've made a good beginning?" She nodded encouragingly. "Are you all right?" he said, looking into her face.

"Yes," she answered, "but I'm cold."

"Cold?—to-night?"

She shook her head. "Not really. . . . Shivery. . . . Feel."

At table, she talked to Mrs. Sarrett, but her mind was still taut in the effort of attention she had made, while, on the balcony, Severidge had "said his piece". She had believed at the time that she was scarcely listening, but she must have listened, for she now remembered what he had said. At the outset she had known well enough that he was giving a display, even that it was a customary one; but she no longer held this against him. His energy, his assurance, lulled her, like a comforting drug, and she drank two mouthfuls of her burgundy without sipping it. So great had been his power to project his own mood, that she began to feel now, not only that his performance had been addressed to her but that it had been evoked by her. She was pleased by the flattery of it, knowing it to be flattery.

Mrs. Sarrett was saying that her brother judged all men and even women by their taste in Montrachet, and Vivien, with a challenging smile in acknowledgment of the hint, turned, glass in hand, towards her host and said: "What a wonderful wine, Mr. Severidge! Do you think the Twenty-Nine will be as good?"

[55]

"What a wonderful woman, Mrs. Lerrick!" he answered. "But seriously, what do you know of the Twenty-Nine?"

"Someone told me that it would turn out well. . . . No. I'm not sailing under false colours. I'm not a connoisseur myself."

"But you remembered!" he cried. "Someone told you—but *you* remembered! . . . Lerrick, what have you done to deserve such a wife?"

She saw Henry's eyes turned upon her, and her own hand trembling. She faltered, out of her part, out of her depth; the grinding anxiety of her life rose up like a noise in her brain. For an instant Severidge's grey eyes searched her; then, with a sudden end of his bantering compliments, he gave her time, he deliberately sheltered her retreat. Changing his tone and manner, he said gravely:

"But it isn't about wine that I really want your opinion. You remember what I said, or tried to say, about 'stopping the clock'? Henry quite rightly answered that it was all very well for the chairman of C.M.I., but not so good for a young solicitor. I respect that answer. It—it put me in my place, so to speak, by reminding me that my place is a very exceptional one. But it doesn't exempt Henry or me or you from the root-problem which underlies my little notion of 'stopping the clock'—the problem, I mean, of how, in the modern world, to remain civilized and free—how to avoid becoming an enslaved specialist. The Greeks weren't; the men of the Renaissance weren't; but we are in everlasting danger of it. What is the remedy?"

The question was put to Henry, and took him by surprise. His face, in repose, had been set and drawn. Now he came gallantly to life. "I should have supposed," he said, "that the remedy was not to get into a rut—to cultivate interests outside one's specialization."

To back him up, Vivien spoke without delay, without thought, the first words that came into her head. "I wonder," she said, "whether that's right? It sounds all right as far as it goes, but is it really the answer?"

Severidge did not speak but waited for her. She was grateful, and felt, with a quick warmth of heart, that she had perhaps been unjust to him. His keen, intelligent eyes were looking into hers with genuine seriousness and expectation. She took a sudden grasp of the subject, became interested in it.

"I believe," she said, "that being civilized and free depends on having something inside yourself to be true to—and on knowing what that something is." Speaking at first rapidly and almost wildly, then with increasing calm, she explained that, when she was at school, and afterwards, she had cared for music more than for anything else in the world, and that, though she hadn't "given it up", she hadn't really developed her knowledge of it, and now—she was a good amateur.

"But that's something," Severidge said. "Isn't that being civilized?"

"Yes," she answered, "it's something. It gives me a great deal of happiness, but I think I should have been more, not less, civilized if I had gone deeper into music and——"

"Does that apply to me and to Henry?" Severidge asked. "If I go deeper and deeper into my job and he into his, and if we don't cultivate interests outside them, is that the way of salvation?"

"If your job is *really* your job," she said, "then I think so."

"You mean that I ought to cut myself off from interests outside it? Surely——"

"Not 'cut yourself off'. No. . . . But you see," she continued, "the outside interests can be either an enrichment or a dissipation. Either you have a home and go out exploring and bring back treasures from foreign parts or—you're just a rolling stone. Either the outside interests add something to you, or they take *you* away. If I had gone really deep into my music, then——"

"Then," Mrs. Sarrett put in, "all things would have been added unto you. I understand perfectly. So would George if he were a Christian."

Vivien nodded and threw back her head. Severidge, fascinated by her breathlessness, watched the little pulse at the base of her throat and caressed his wine-glass with agile fingers from bowl to stem, from stem to bowl.

"Of course," she said, "if you think of it as 'getting into the rut of your specialization', then it sounds wrong. But that's only because a 'rut' is shallow and so the whole thing is made to sound shallow. But Beethoven's rut wasn't shallow. And if you think of it as going deeper and deeper into your own real job—being more and more true to yourself—then the 'outside interests' themselves don't remain 'outside'; they come in; they contribute. They make you richer because you are already rich. But if you cultivate them *as* outside interests—I mean, if you 'take up' painting or 'take up' sociology or even religion—then they only scatter you: they make you poorer because you are already poor."

She leaned back in her chair, and her mind said: To-morrow Henry must tell Gasky, or shall I? . . . There was a moment's silence.

"The pure milk of individualism!" Severidge exclaimed.

They were still silent.

"The pure milk of Christianity," Mrs. Sarrett remarked. " 'For he that hath to him shall be given, and he that hath not from him shall be taken even that which he hath.' "

"My dear Molly," her brother said, "you and your texts!" Then to Vivien: "Are you a Christian?" But he did not wait for her answer and continued. "You know, the whole tendency of modern thought is against you. I am against you, I confess. Of course, if by 'outside interests' one means 'taking up' this or that in an amateur way—going to lectures spasmodically and picking up scraps of knowledge from Outlines and Child's Guides—then what you say is right enough: it is just frittering life away. But there's another aspect of the matter. Here's the world in the devil of a mess—are we going to do nothing about it? Am I to sit in C.M.I. making money or you at your piano making music, and not recognize that one of the so-called 'outside interests' is the suffering of the common man—housing, unemployment, all the rest of it? The tendency of the modern world is towards collective action. You say that a man's whole job is to be truer and truer to himself. I hate that doctrine. In any case, I say that a man is true to himself when he is true to the community. I say: 'I am because the community is'. What is the answer to that?"

Vivien said: "Either a very long answer or a very short one."

"What is the short one?"

"I suppose a man would give it who said: 'I am because the kingdom of God is within me', meaning, by 'the kingdom of God', whatever inside himself he recognized as being——"

"But listen," Severidge interrupted, "this is the twentieth century: have you noticed what has happened in Germany and Russia?"

"Yes," she said, "and in Babylon and in Tyre."

Up went his eyebrows. "Wasn't I right, Molly, to stop the clock this evening? This is an occasion!" He laughed the delighted, vigorous laugh of a young man. "Nothing is pleasanter than to be defeated in debate by a beautiful lady. Which is she—a century behind her time or a century in advance of it?" Then, of Vivien herself, he asked: "But won't you admit that your line is anti-social? The modern conscience is a social conscience where there is any conscience at all."

"No," she said, "I'm not anti-social. It's a question of whether I can be of any good to society unless I am of some real good in myself. It comes back to your own problem—how to be in your own way (and everyone's way is different) civilized and free. For me that seems to come first."

"I'm sorry, George," Mrs. Sarrett put in, "but I have another of my quotations."

"Which is?" he asked with polite impatience.

" 'Seek ye *first* the kingdom of God.' "

He brushed this aside. What pleased him was that he had drawn Vivien out; he was excited by her unguardedness, by the fact of her having given herself away, by the colour that her thought had summoned to her cheeks and by the sudden thirst with which she drank wine. In this mood, there was no question she would not answer with the rash promptness of a brilliant student.

But he did not press her yet. To do so would have been to alarm her into calling up her reserves, and he turned deliberately from her to Henry who was astute enough to bring up again the question of the Cennini manuscript about which his host, with evident pride and interest, had been telling him when Vivien had intervened.

"Ah, yes," Severidge said, "I was in the middle of telling you about Cennini when we were plunged so charmingly into the pure milk of individualism." and he described Cennino Cennini's *Treatise* on painting, saying that Cennini himself was a painter who lived at the end of the fourteenth and the beginning of the fifteenth century and inherited, by a direct line of teachers, the tradition of Giotto. But none of his own paintings survived. He was known by his *Treatise* only, partly because it was of immense value historically, partly because it had an endearing grace and humour. There were three early manuscripts of it, two Florentine, one in the Vatican, and now a fourth had turned up in the house of a certain Mrs. Gorsand, twenty miles from Glasgow. "I heard of its existence when I was in Tours three years ago," Severidge said. "In a *château* in that part of the world there was a fifteenth-century record of it and a tradition of its having gone with a bride of the family to Scotland. The Scottish name was known and that Scottish family very much exists; the head of it is on my Board. But they had never heard of Cennini and in their library there wasn't a sniff of him except an entry in a catalogue dated 1827. All I knew was that he was there then and gone now."

"But you found him?" Henry asked.

"I found him," Severidge answered, "but not at first. I put the genealogists on to the track. The Scots are pretty careful of their family trees. Follow the branches and follow the twigs; follow the wills. Not that people catalogue all the books they bequeath, but there was a chance for this one. Persistence and a bit of luck will find most things in this world. But in fact the search failed until this spring when the manuscript itself appeared on loan in an exhibition. The owner is Mrs. Gorsand. She turns out to be a widow come down in the world—a very distant twig of that noble family tree, but the Cennini is proof of her connexion with the trunk, it's a symbol of her departed glory, and nothing will make her part with it, though I dare say it would buy everything else she possesses in the world. Nothing will make her part with it—or so she says now."

"The Scots are pretty stubborn," Henry answered.

"May be, but money humanizes them in the end as it does everyone else. . . . Now tell me, if you wanted that manuscript, how would you go about it?"

Henry considered. "Well, I shouldn't just bid her up. Threaten a Scot and he digs his heels in. . . . I should try a different kind of persuasion."

Severidge concentrated his attention. "Ah, you would, would you?"

"If she liked me, for example," Henry said, "if she thought I genuinely prized the thing and should be—well, worthy of it, if you see what I mean, then it might smooth the way. Or there's another possibility—but that would depend on what I wanted it for." He looked up from the apple he had been peeling and said: "What do you want it for? Why do you want it?"

"What do you mean: why do I want it?"

"Well," said Henry, "there might be a dozen reasons. To sell again. Or to be the envy of other collectors. Or because you really want it for its own sake. Or——"

"That's too subtle for me," Severidge interrupted with the smile of a plain man for such youthful hair-splitting. "Let's say just 'to have it'. What then?"

Henry smiled. His mind said: That isn't an answer; anyhow not yours; but he was discreet enough not to make his challenge. "What I was thinking," he replied, "was that the old lady might be brought much nearer to parting with it if she were told, let's say, that ultimately it would go to the British Museum or some Scottish collection. I mean, in that way her pride——"

"No," Severidge interrupted, "that won't do. If I *were* going to leave it to the British Museum, or back into her own precious family, I wouldn't tell her so for all the world. That wouldn't be fair."

"Fair?" Vivien asked.

"Oh no," Severidge answered, disregarding her and keeping his eyes on Henry, "I don't want to persuade her with inducements of that sort. This must be a straight bargain and no nonsense about it."

He made it sound as if he were refusing to cheat Mrs. Gorsand, and Vivien saw that this was, indeed, what at that moment he himself believed.

"None of that!" he continued with the strange, almost soundless laugh that expressed the embarrassments of his soul. "Your other idea was much better. If you could make her *like* you so that when she saw the colour of your money she could say to herself that— You see the point? Everyone who surrenders has to have an excuse at the moment of surrender; to give him the excuse is good business. The truth comes home afterwards."

"Why don't you let the old lady keep her manuscript?" Vivien asked. "You don't really want it."

"Oh yes, I do!" Severidge exclaimed, and his mind echoed him silently: Oh yes, I do—while *she* wants it; and, hearing this echo in his mind, he raised his voice as if to drown it and said to Henry: "Look. Here's a proposition. I believe in letting men follow up their own ideas. You go up to Glasgow—professionally, of course—and come back with Cennini or, if you don't come back with it, fix the price, prepare the way for me. Later I'll go up myself and take the surrender."

Vivien looked at Henry to see whether the word "surrender" had made its mark upon him; but Henry's mind was elsewhere.

"Of course, I'll go gladly," he said, thinking that Humphrey Waynford would postpone their engagement without hesitation; he wouldn't stand in the way of a job for C.M.I. More than that, he would be valuably impressed by the appearance of this gigantic client. "I'll go like a shot and do what I can. The only thing is——"

"What? You can postpone anything else. Go up to-morrow by the night train. See her Thursday. Stay the week-end if necessary."

"There's no difficulty about that," Henry said. "The only

thing is—to go up suddenly looks like being a bit eager, doesn't it? It might put up the price."

"A good point," Severidge acknowledged. Then, as Henry had expected, he put the objection aside. "Don't you worry about that. I'll give you a limit to-morrow. You go and do what you can. A delicate negotiation. Rather a test in a way."

After dinner, they returned to the balcony. The discussion of one book led easily to discussion of another, and Severidge was able to confirm his belief that it was Vivien's mother who had yielded Gaskony his *Marius*. Therefore, it was Vivien's mother whom Gaskony had wished to be his wife. And that, Severidge reflected, makes the book an exceedingly precious possession for a man of Gaskony's type. It is his memory. It is his integrity. . . . But with this matter he was not immediately concerned. He had, he told himself, talked of Gaskony enough; Vivien was beginning to jib at the subject, and he switched out the light that his mind was playing upon it.

12

HE switched it out as one switches out the light in a room in which one remains. The room is no longer visible but it is still there.

Severidge had what certain barristers, who apply the same capacity to their many briefs, recognize as the gift of a "compartment-mind". This, with his power to make precise estimate of other men's greeds, to know intuitively how much they would pay and in what forms they would least reluctantly make payment, was the root of his success. Without the gift of a compartment-mind, he could not have harvested the fruit of his other talents; he would have become confused or have been driven mad by overwork and the cumulative anxiety of many decisions. In fact, his anxieties did not accumulate; while he gave his mind to one problem, he excluded all others. The gift of a compartment-mind was the order, the sanity and the enablement of his genius. It was this because, in business, it was perfect; but, in his personal life, it was imperfect. In business, when he passed from one subject to another, he did not switch off the light in a compartment of thought and yet remain in that compartment; instead he proceeded mentally from one well-lighted room to another, shutting the door firmly behind him; the room he had left ceased to exist for him until he chose to re-enter it. But when, in a room of his own soul, he switched off the light, the room was still there. His consciousness of being in it receded, but continued nevertheless.

For this reason, though he wished to enjoy the company of his guests for its own sake, he was unable to separate this enjoyment from his knowledge that Vivien, being the daughter of the woman whom Gaskony had loved, was Gaskony's chief hostage to Fortune. She was what fools would call the Judge's "sentimentality". That was to miss the point. She was much more than his "sentimentality"; she was that perilous thing—his self-symb ; through her, his single-mindedness was vulnerable. And S ridge was well aware that to-night she herself was outs er defences; she and Henry were like a cry suppresse n might become suddenly an uncontrol-lable scream it was it—a quarrel? Much more. The girl was half- with wine, but with anguish, as men can be drun lessness; as they talk with feverish lucidity to ke awake, so was she talking to keep at bay som ome breaking-up of her life; and Severidge ha disintegration.

nd Henry to talk about themselves. To lead or reasons of vanity, he began to talk about o autobiography by way of music, education, mes, for Henry was interested in games. He as he had often found before, that he could imself in his sister's presence. When he rose, doctor had ordered her to keep very early berated, and, when she was gone, he sighed lease of the evening. And yet he could not re. The balcony reminded him of the deck of wn, of the Aegean.

vas calm. Above the house-tops, light cloud the stars without obscuring them, and his im-ed outward from the city.

ts," he said, shifting in his chair and stretching ve his head, "that the sky goes down to the he said this, he heard the wash of the Aegean, moon's track upon the waves. The Judge was at guest, his captive; and he thought: But I am a man I wish no harm to anyone. Looking at Vivien, he y for the suffering he saw in a face so beautiful and t sorry for the young man too. He would have liked em; he would have liked to preserve them from

[65]

harm, to take nothing from them, to take nothing from the world. Swept by this gust of innocence, he was on the point of saying aloud: "Don't go to Glasgow. I'll drop Cennini. I won't disturb the old lady," but he did not; he found it easier to say to Henry: "You told me you were happy at school. Why were you? How do you account for it? It interests me."

"Well, I don't know," Henry began. "Probably games. Besides I got my cricket-cap early. I got it while I was still in the Lower School. That puts you on top of the world."

"And would you give that simple reason?" Severidge asked Vivien. "Pobably you know your husband better than he knows himself. Why was he happy? If it comes to that, why is he?"

Laying her hand on Henry's arm, Vivien said: "He's very much all-of-a-piece. Not on the surface," she added with a laugh. "On the surface, he's a very erratic creature. But deep down, he's all-of-a-piece. Is that true, Henry? . . . But, of course, you wouldn't know!"

He laughed back at her. "Darling, I expect I am what you say I am. But have I got a deep-down? Anyhow at the moment it's nice of you to say so."

"And now," said Severidge, "are you all-of-a-piece?"

Before Henry could speak, Vivien increased her pressure on his arm and replied: "Yes, we are. I'm sure we are."

"Bless you," Severidge answered, taking breath, "that's good to hear," and the tone of sincerity that he heard in his own voice gave him so much reassurance that there, perhaps, he might have left it if Vivien had not said:

"I suppose I told a lie about my music just now."

"You mean, it's better than——"

"I mean it was probably much less *me* than I thought it was."

As she said this, she was neither looking at that imperfect creature her husband, nor touching him. She was far back in her chair, drawing in the smoke from a cigarette that he had just lighted for her. But her mind, recalled to their earliest days together and to her imagining of him in the years of his boyhood and youth, was full of the hopelessness of their present position and of her love for him. She was happier in her marriage for all its stress than she had been in her music, and Severidge, who always knew what any man would pay and in what form he would make payment, said within him: so it is in their marriage that they are true to themselves, this charming and ill-assorted pair! and he knew at once that, in all his relationship with them, he would never doubt this, would never be able to doubt or forget it. It was already written indelibly, as a fact, in the card-index of his judgments, and he began to desire the girl, not frivolously and casually, nor with a lascivious hunger, but with the desire of the deaf for hearing as they watch the movement of a stream. He desired the marriage, which was the girl's integrity, rather than the girl herself. It presented itself to him as a great sheet of paper may present itself to a man who is not an artist—as a reproach and challenge to his incapacity, as something to be scrawled upon.

He was aware that, in reason, this marriage was an unsuitable one. Certainly so strange a partnership was full of stress. Nevertheless, when Henry had been asked: "Are you all-of-a-piece?" and she, intervening, had replied: "Yes, we are," she had borne witness, not to a working agreement, a compromise of effect, but to a truth that was for her absolute, and would survive all infidelities to it because it was an inalienable part of herself. By it, Severidge knew, he was separated from her, as the deaf are from sound, and as he had always been separated from any man who had within him a truth to which to be true—a core, a stem, a root, an earth, and who was not an effect only.

Severidge, rich in intellect, vigorous and skilful in action, not without benevolence, was spiritually without core. To the question: "What do I do? What do I produce?" there was an honourable, well-wishing, effective answer, at any rate an answer in conscience—for this was the scope of his conscience; but to the question: "Who am I?" there was none. Many human beings have no knowledge of themselves except as effects. They carry within them no reconciliation of these effects, no sense of a realized or realizable individuality, no origin of the notes they give out. They are neither musicians nor children singing; they are gramophones, mass-produced—effect-makers, good or bad. Of these, some are content, as

Severidge was not; they think complacently in terms of effect, as a gramophone might be supposed to think as it came off the production-line. But some are unhappy as a gramophone might be which was aware of music's cause and that it was itself empty of this cause. Severidge resembled such a gramophone. In business, his effect-making had a perfection which, like all perfection in its own kind, was beautiful, and, while he exercised this faculty, he had a sense of flawlessness, of innocence. He felt then: I am a good man, as a gramophone might feel: I am a good gramophone. But, observing others at school and in later life, he had found that certain men were to him what musicians are to gramophones—often extremely incompetent, but still musicians, aware of music within them; often untrue to their truth but recognizing it as theirs, their very own, the nature of their being, their stem, root and seed, their link with Earth, their unity with Nature, their not-being-lonely, their not-being-sterile-or-dead.

Severidge could not endure, in others, this inward dedication. He did not hate those who were conscious of it, but hated that in them which excluded him. He did not wish to harm or destroy, but to penetrate.

"If your music is less to you than you thought," he asked now, "what do you put in its place?"

She was silent, but he knew the answer. In his presence, she turned away from it, as Gaskony always turned away, as all men and women who had an answer turned away from him who had none.

"If you are to speak of being true to yourself," he persisted, "there must be something to which you are true. What is it? Music? Religion? What? . . . Well, you don't answer that question. But you'd answer it to the Judge, wouldn't you?"

"I think he'd take the answer for granted."

Severidge shrugged his shoulders. "I don't blame you. People who are sure of themselves—aristocrats or peasants—don't analyse their breed. They feel it inside them—and there it is. . . . Anyhow I know you can't answer the question to me. . . . My receiver's off."

[68]

The last three words, and the unrelenting candour with which they were spoken, astonished and frightened her. Henry laughed aloud.

"I doubt," he said, "whether there's much you miss."

"Oh yes, there is," Severidge answered almost jocularly. "You ask your wife. You ask the Judge. There's a great deal I miss. The really remarkable thing about me is that I know it. It's as if a chap, lying in his grave, were to hear people making love or singing hymns above his head and were to say to himself: "What is it—day or night?"

"You mean—jealous?" Henry said.

"No," Severidge answered, his eyes on the inner curve of Vivien's arm, "not in the least. But wanting to be among them— to find out. That's why ghosts walk, I expect." He stood up, moved to the railing of the balcony and leaned against it, looking down.

"It's getting chilly. Let's go in and shut the glass doors. Vivien shall play to us. . . . You know," he continued, taking her hand for a moment as he led her indoors, "what you call being 'all-of-a-piece' puzzles me. You understand it; so does the Judge. I have to remind myself that you are not his daughter."

"But we are not alike."

"Yes, you are. In many ways. . . . Among others, you both like to be taken charge of. Isn't that true?"

"Very true."

"And both of you need it for the same reason—not that you're incompetent or lazy, but because in your hearts what you want is a chance—well, you may choose the phrase—I can only say: to be all-of-a-piece? to be true to yourselves? to cultivate your garden?"

"You know a lot," she replied.

"A lot," he said, "but not enough. I know people have gardens of that kind but I haven't one myself. . . . There, now sit down at that Steinway and play a little in what might have been your garden if you hadn't chosen another."

She looked at Henry who was busily lighting candles; then

at Severidge, with acknowledgment of his insight, his power of self-criticism, with gratitude for his gentleness towards her personally, with an emotion, half of fear, half of admiration, stirred in her by the hard thrust of his curiosity, and, at the same time, a sense of his being excessive and, even, a little ridiculous. Ridiculous, but formidable. She herself was excited and confused. Music, when she began to play, would, she knew, resolve the conflict of her moods—would "sort her out", and she lifted her hands to the keys. Then she remembered the Waynford Trustees and that Henry needed twelve, or was it sixteen, thousand pounds, and that one morning he would come out of prison. She would take the car to meet him— but she would have no car. She would take a taxi to meet him and he would look at her, wondering whether to be gay or sad. They would eat food together, though neither wanted it, because food and drink bridge the gaps in life. At table they would look at each other's hands.

Meanwhile she had played the two opening bars of a mazurka of Chopin. She looked down at her hands and withdrew them on to her lap.

Severidge did not expostulate politely but accepted at once that she would not play. "Is that garden shut?" he said with protective abruptness. "What do you want to do, then? Take out a car and drive?"

"What made you think of that?"

He rose with an eager, springy movement. "Henry, what do you say?"

Henry agreed. They went out. Severidge drove. Henry sat in the back seat.

"Where are we going?" Vivien asked.

"Lean back and don't talk for a bit," Severidge answered. "And don't worry. In an hour, I'll bring you back to my door. Or I'll drive you to Hadscombe and send your own car down to-morrow. Shut your eyes." Over his shoulder he said to Henry: "I shall have to do a bit of thinking before I give you a limit for the Cennini. There isn't a market price for a commodity that changes hands twice in five hundred years."

13

On the evening of the following day at seven o'clock the Judge was seated, in an attitude of uncomfortable alertness, on the leather-topped fender of his living-room in the Temple. He had been in this position since Henry left him more than an hour earlier. His fingers had not shifted their grasp on the brass edges of the fender. He looked at them now, his palms outspread. A blue line of pressure ran across them. They were cold and stiff. He began to work them, slowly clawing the air, to restore the circulation of the blood.

Henry had told him the truth. At first, not all of it, but the Judge was satisfied that the whole truth had come out in the end. They had squared themselves to table with ink and paper and totted it up. What it came to was that twenty-three thousand were needed urgently to keep Henry from exposure and prison, and another three soon.

Quite hopeless. Henry himself had seen this without being told. "I haven't come here to borrow, Gasky. You haven't got it; I know that. I've come because Vivien wanted you to be told the worst." The Judge had nevertheless brought down from a shelf a list of his investments. A good parcel of his savings (and he had never been much of a saver) had gone to Vivien's marriage settlement and that wasn't to be touched—indeed it was so tied up that it couldn't be touched in her lifetime even with her consent. What remained to him was a pleasant little nest-egg; the income from it, added to his pension, gave him all he wanted—more, perhaps, than he needed. He could cut down, and would. To keep Vivien's husband out of gaol, he would cut down drastically. But by far the greater part of what he had came to him as pension. To save out of that would need time and there was no time. Matched with Henry's disaster, the possessions he could sell were a fleabite. "I could help a bit," he had said, "but all I could do wouldn't save you."

"I know," Henry had answered. "It would only be pouring good money after bad. If I'm to go to prison, I might as well go there at the expense of the Waynford Trustees—not at yours."

Then he had gone off to Hadscombe to see Vivien and pack a suitcase. This evening he would go to Scotland by the night train—on a job for Severidge.

The Judge looked about him at the room in which Henry had told him what there was to tell—at the list of investments still lying on the table, at the chair standing askew as Henry had pushed it back, and at the permanent, inanimate things— the ormolu clock, the small bronzes that flanked it, his arm-chair, and the book he had been reading when Henry entered— all of which seemed now to belong to a lost, arcadian period of his life separated from him by the torrent of disaster suddenly released. When ill news comes, inanimate things, which re-main unaffected by it, seem to retain in themselves the ghost of the observer's lost happiness; he touches the clock, half-expecting from it a miraculous response; he takes up again the discarded book, remembering—*this* was the paragraph half-finished when disaster struck; and they give back nothing. So Gaskony's mind had wandered from chair to table, from curtain to rug, when Julia died; so it wandered now, until solitude in that familiar room became intolerable to him. Though the evening was warm, he put on a light overcoat before going out.

At Rodd's he chose a side-table at which to dine alone—a rare choice for him who loved company, an inwardly reluctant choice, too, for he had come from the Temple to avoid solitude; yet he made it because—well, was it only because it was a Victorian convention to hug your griefs, to pull a long face, to go into a corner to blubber? Gaskony, naturally cheerful, a hater of shams, no great admirer of dignity for dignity's sake, began to think, as he sat at the side-table waiting for his soup: Life has to be lived though the heavens fall; I don't help Henry or Vivien or myself by cutting myself off from my fellowmen and grouching in a corner like a tragedy-queen who must have the stage to herself until she has done with her mourning! and he looked up from the bread he was crumbling to notice Severidge at the cashier's desk paying for an early meal. He watched Severidge, and, in a perversity of mood, hailed him.

"Severidge!"

The hail was answered with the readiest affability. They said the day was hot but had cooled off towards evening.

"And my boy," said the Judge, "I call him 'my boy' you know—I mean young Lerrick—tells me you have been kind enough to give him a job. Good of you after that little brush we had when last we met."

"Good Lord," said Severidge, "the fault was mine. . . . As for the Glasgow job, I assure you I was acting in my own interest. Henry had ideas about it. I think he can do what I want. Anyhow, he'll make an intelligent shot at it. . . . Hey, Dunstable!"— this to the wine-steward who was passing by with a decanter— "give me my port here. I'll take it at Sir William's table. . . . May I?"

"Of course," said the Judge, "delighted." What on earth had made him call Severidge? What had made him speak of Henry?

"Queer," he said aloud.

"What's queer?"

If the Judge had answered truly, he would have said: Queer that I should be glad even of your company tonight! Anything human. Any talk. Anything to stop the mental adding up of impossible sums. . . . Fortunately there was no need to answer at all. Severidge was sitting down and silently watching the port flow from decanter to glass.

"One good service you've done me," Severidge began.

"Indeed? What?"

"Put me on to reading that book, *Marius the Epicurean*, again."

Instantly the Judge was on his guard, but he said: "Ah! I'm glad."

"You don't sound glad! You sound jealous," Severidge replied in a tone of gentle teasing. "You haven't the copyright, you know, Judge!"

Gaskony smiled, ate his soup and said only: "No, I don't claim that that was included in the purchase price."

" 'Price'? But—" Severidge paused discreetly. "I don't want to go back over old ground," he continued, "but, in fact, didn't you tell me the book was a gift?"

"So it was. So it was. All the same—no matter, why—I paid over my eight-and-six. You see—well, no matter. . . . Anyhow, I was a young barrister. Briefless. Eight-and-six was a lot of money then."

Severidge then spoke wisely. "That alone would make the book precious."

"Quite right," said the Judge. "How did you know that?"

"And why shouldn't I?"

"You have never been poor."

"For that matter, Shakespeare had never been a Jew. . . . There's a bit of Shakespeare that always sticks in my mind." The Judge laid down his spoon, and Severidge continued: "It's in *The Merchant*. You remember—when Shylock's daughter has run away and he is told that she's spending money like water in Genoa?"

"Yes," the Judge said, "go on."

"And Tubal tells him that she gave a ring in exchange for a monkey? . . . It's Shylock's answer that I remember: 'It was my turquoise; I had it of Leah when I was a bachelor: I would not have given it for a wilderness of monkeys.' "

The Judge made no reply until at last he said: "Turquoise. Not a costly ring."

"I can tell you what it cost."

At this the Judge turned his head. "Can you? Shylock doesn't say, as I recollect."

"It cost eight-and-six. Which is why, if I were to offer you eight pounds ten for *Marius*, you would say——"

"Precisely," the Judge interrupted. "Shakespeare knew his job."

"Or twenty-five pounds. Or two-fifty."

The Judge drew his hand over his nose. "Or a wilderness of——"

Severidge opened his mouth to a breathy, soundless laugh—an awkward gasping. "In fact," he said, "to prove a point that interests me, I do now seriously offer you two hundred and fifty pounds for your copy of *Marius*."

"Nonsense," Gaskony answered.

"It's a firm offer."

Gaskony looked into his face. The offer was firm enough, but he chose not to regard it so. "What a loyal Shakespearian you are! My answer would still be Shylock's."

"Precisely," Severidge said. "I was proving my point."

"Mm . . . yes . . . an interesting point," the Judge said. He took a mouthful of omelette; it was a good omelette, but he had no stomach for it and sent it away. "Bring me some coffee."

"The joint's very good, Sir William. Underdone."

"No. . . . Coffee. . . . I want to smoke."

14

AFTER his first meeting with Mrs. Gorsand on Thursday afternoon, Henry telegraphed: "Not very encouraging but not
hopeless. Propose stay week-end Glasgow. Please tell my wife."

Severidge picked up his house-telephone. "I want Mrs.
Henry Lerrick, the Red House, Hadscombe. On my own line.
I'll speak myself."

He gave her Henry's message.

"I do hope he pulls it off," she said.

"Why so anxious?"

"Only that there are times when to—to succeed in something is important. This is his first job for C.M.I."

Severidge forbore from saying that it wasn't C.M.I. that
coveted the widow Gorsand's manuscript. I suppose, he said
to himself, when they got home, they talked about this Glasgow
job as a golden opportunity. Young. Happy. Life the hell of a
romantic progress. Worried about something. Then this chance.
One forgets that; and he said into the telephone: "Look. You'll
be alone this week-end. Why not spend it with my sister and
me in the country? I could drive you down on Friday evening;
bring you back Monday morning."

Vivien said she would go. The invitation gave her the feeling
of security, of not being idle and outcast, which at that time
she most needed, and she wrote a short note to the Judge
telling him her movements and ending: "Perhaps things will
clear themselves up somehow. Anyhow, you shan't be worried
any more with our troubles until after the week-end." She
took this out to the post-office and there sent a telegram
to Henry full of the words which were pledges and tokens

between them—an assurance of her love that he alone would understand.

Severidge's house, Felden Lodge, looked out from a wooded hillside on to the village of Felden in Oxfordshire. The weather was clear, and Vivien could see from her bedroom window the gleam of the Thames and the spires of Oxford itself. Except Mrs. Sarrett, who kept house for her brother in the country, no one was there but Severidge and Vivien herself, and Severidge did not press his company upon her. She was increasingly at ease with him; she enjoyed her exploration of his library, her dips in his swimming-pool, and her morning hours, which he did not interrupt, at his piano.

"Listen," he had said on the first evening, when Mrs. Sarrett had gone to bed and Vivien was about to follow, "I'll be perfectly frank. What is troubling you I don't know and I don't ask; but whatever it is, why not try the effect of stopping the clock? While you're here, nothing and no one shall get at you—neither I nor anyone else. You have two clear days. Put a bracket round them."

This she could not do; nor did she attempt it. The core of her life was in her marriage; while Henry was in peril, she could not rest; but, amid the conflict of her anxieties, she did in those days find a balance; she took courage to face whatever might come and drove panic out. On Saturday morning there was a letter from Gasky. She opened it at breakfast, swiftly refolded it and put it away unread, knowing that the handwriting had not escaped Severidge's eye. When she was alone, she found that the letter was looking towards the future, an assurance that even this disaster was to be lived through and lived down; it contained no present remedy; he could sell certain securities, but they would, he said, "by no means fill poor Henry's bucket and, in this case, only a full bucket is of any good." Then he added:

But I will say, Vivien, I never liked your Henry better than I did yesterday evening when he told me that story.

Others—and we have to face that fact—will not see any extenuating circumstances, and I am not sure that I see many, but what I did see was a man who did not whine or shift the blame and who convinced me at any rate that, in spite of the plain dishonesty of what he had done, he was not at root dishonest. Sometimes one feels that it won't really help if a man does get out of deep water—he will only tumble in again. Henry won't, and that puts a different face on the thing. But I am only telling you what, I am sure, you already know. Nevertheless, it may be worth my saying it. The longer I live in this morally indignant world where people organize their grievances in self-righteous groups—pressure-groups, leagues, bunds, confederations, full of hatred and scorn and blame, grasping, aggressive, whining for their infernal rights—the more certain I am that only personal relationships matter in the end. Group-thinking is ultimately valueless because groups can't think except in terms of effect. Stick to a man for the sake of what he is, regardless of what he happens to have done, and, when you are old, you won't be sorry.

Vivien read this with full assent. She believed that the act of forgiveness, though required of friends, was not required of lovers, for love was unconditional; its forgiveness was prospective and infinite; by its coming to life and the inclusion of two identities in it, the whole future of each was, by the other, finally redeemed. This was the test of love, its distinction from sentiment or passion other than itself. If, between lovers, this mutual redemption was imperfect, it was imperfect because their identities, though included by their love, were not fused in it; but suffering, she thought, may bring fusion nearer; I don't know, but I think it may if it doesn't divide us, if only I can keep touch while he is in prison.

She came in from the garden, where she had read the Judge's letter, and, while she was tearing it into small fragments, a telegram was brought in answer to hers. It seemed also an answer to her thoughts, and she went through the day in the comfort of it. After tea she swam, and dressed early. Severidge came from the house and sat beside her on a small, circular terrace, ringed with flowers, which he called the Bastion. They spoke of the Civil War and of the cavalry skirmish at Islip, not far away. "One of our guests coming in to dine this evening—old Bill Hetherigg—had an ancestor wounded there," Severidge told her, "and Bill's sister, with the excellent name of Sophia, has one of those long faces that look out of Stuart portraits—seem to have been thought beautiful then. One of the reasons that I like the Hetheriggs is that they are always smiling and imperturbable—urbane is the word. They live up to their family's motto. I forget the Latin. Hetherigg translates it: 'The world is older'."

" 'The world is older,' " Vivien repeated. "Older than what?"

"Than one's hopes. . . . Than one's troubles."

She smiled. "That's a Cockney motto too: 'It will all be the same in a hundred years'." Then she asked: "Did you bring in the Hetheriggs and their motto just for the sake of comforting me?"

"No," he answered, "not altogether. Your troubles, whatever they are—I was going to say they are no affair of mine: I'd rather say I have no claim to them. Though if it would help you to talk, I wish you would. From your point of view, I have the advantage of being more or less a stranger. It's sometimes easier to talk to them."

He spoke with so steady a confidence that she had an impulse, almost overwhelming, to tell him the truth. It would have been unspeakable relief. A fantasy presented itself to her of his going into the house and returning with a cheque that would break the walls of her mental prison, and she heard herself, on the telephone to Glasgow, saying: It's all right, Henry. Don't ask how or why. My darling, it's all right. . . . A fantasy? Was it impossible in Severidge's present mood? She looked at him, her lips parted. At that instant he leaned forward and cocked his ear for the confession, and she recoiled.

"Rather a dull trouble," was all she said. "Only that we have been extravagant, and ought to sell our house, and——" but she said no more.

Severidge took defeat patiently and covered even his knowledge of it. He spoke with sympathy of the trouble of disrupting their home and asked where they proposed to live; then dropped the subject.

"Isn't it about time," he said, "that drinks were coming out?" and looked away from her, over his shoulder, towards the house.

Neither that evening nor on Sunday did he make any attempt to come near to her secret, but won back her confidence by many personal kindnesses of word, of deed, and even, she could not but believe, of thought. There was a certain awkwardness in his goodwill, a shyness—and a corresponding abruptness—of approach, as though he were made clumsy by the effort to abstain from her. He, who had so much confidence different in kind, had not the graceful confidence of breeding; but she did not take account of this; except at rare moments, which she smiled at, and discounted, she was not sexually aware of him; and she liked his company because his life was firm, and so great a margin lay between him and danger. Yet when it appeared in the evening that he intended to go to church, she was touched coldly by the finger of the incongruous. Church-going was his custom when at Felden; he made no show of piety but went, without hypocritical pretence, because his local position required it of him. Mrs. Sarrett and Vivien went also, and Laurence Sarrett, a long-necked, red-haired youth of eighteen, grotesquely unlike his mother, who was "working up from the bottom" in the C.M.I. works thirty miles away and had come home for Sunday night. His large hands were laced, in the skin-creases, with an irremovable grime; he hid them when he could, looked at his uncle like a frightened giant, and, finding that Vivien was willing to meet him on his own ground, poured out to her his passion for chemistry and his desire to climb mountains. In church he sat between her and his mother, and found the place for her in the hymn-book.

Severidge was divided from her by the length of the pew.

At first she forgot him and prayed for Henry's and her own deliverance, but, as the Service continued, her mind was distracted by him. He kneeled in the attitude of prayer on a high box-hassock, and his bent knees, in their tautened dark-blue cloth, remained visible when she shut her eyes; she began to fight against her knowledge of his presence, but it prevailed upon her more and more as though it were his will that it should prevail. Even the prayer she loved most passed without her hearing it; she found that it was gone; she tried to recover it and, while the sermon was beginning, to read it to herself—"Lighten our darkness, we beseech Thee, O Lord"—but she could not. The Rector was giving out his text from the eleventh chapter of Luke:

"Then goeth he, and taketh to him seven other spirits more wicked than himself; and they enter in, and dwell there: and the last state of that man is worse than the first."

Never before had she heard a sermon on evil spirits; but the Rector was old and fearless; he spoke not what would please and flatter, but what he saw. She listened spellbound and was emptied of all thought of Severidge until, walking through the graveyard in the slant of evening, she heard him say behind her in a tone of bitter anger: "Why does the old fool preach such a sermon as that? How many people in Felden, d'you suppose, believe in devils? You might think we were in the Dark Ages. What nonsense it is! Pernicious nonsense, too!"

Vivien drew ahead with Laurence Sarrett. "Tell me," she said, "more about your mountains. You were in the foothills of the Himalayas when we went into church. . . . Let's walk fast. Not by the short cut. Is there another way round?"

"There's a much longer way," the young man said eagerly.

"Let's take it."

"Really? I warn you, it's over two miles."

She looked at the sky and drew breath. "I don't want yet—to go into the house."

Mrs. Sarrett followed more slowly with her brother.

"George," she said, "what are you trying to do with that girl?"

He was angry. "I'm not trying to seduce her, if that's what you mean."

"Not her body, that may be."

"Molly, you're raving mad."

"Still, I love you, George, and, being your sister, I'm not afraid of you. I'm the only person you know on earth of whom either is true. . . . I should leave her alone. I shouldn't even be particularly kind to her if I were you."

"And why shouldn't I be kind to her? What the hell are you driving at?"

"Because she's good; because she's pure in heart. God protects such beings from destruction. They are driven back and back; but they are not lost. It is on their own home that they are driven back. That is God's guidance and mercy."

Severidge looked at her determined, exalted face. "That's all out of my depth," he said, speaking more gently than he had at first, "and I don't see how it applies to me."

"I should leave her alone, George," Mrs. Sarrett repeated. Then she gazed at him: "Why are you so restless? Why are you so unhappy? You always were, even when you were a boy."

15

HENRY reached London on Monday morning. On Sunday at luncheon Mrs. Gorsand had agreed to sell and at a price below Severidge's limit. The manner of it had been surprising.

The meal had been sparse. When it was over, they withdrew from table no farther than to a couple of upright chairs which stood in a pinched bay-window looking on to the street. Between them was a bamboo table and on the table the model of a ship under a glass cover, for Mrs. Gorsand's husband had been a sea-captain. Mrs. Gorsand was of great age but her cheeks were still high and rounded; the prettiness of her youth lingered; she was taut and spry. Beneath the collar of her dress, which was hooked up to the throat, she wore a brooch of sadonyx on which a woman's head was cut. She would often lay her fingers on this brooch and sometimes unpin it and hold it between her hands.

"How pleasant it is," she said, "when the sun falls down the street. One catches it now; at tea-time it will be behind the roofs. . . . But you have come again to talk business," she continued abruptly. "It means much to you, young man, that I should agree?"

"I confess it does."

"How much?"

By this Henry was taken aback.

"I mean," said the widow, "how much in commission?"

"Oh," he answered with a broad grin, "nothing in commission, unfortunately."

"What do you get out of it, then?"

"A fee and expenses."

"Is that all?"

"That—and the chance it gives me. Mr. Severidge is the—well, Mr. Severidge, in his own line of business, is——"

"Go on, go on, young man. Say what you have to say in your own language."

"I was going to say he's the hell of a big gun, and this is my first job for him. I think he's taken to us a bit, so naturally if I pull this off——"

" 'Us'?"

"My wife and me."

The old lady tapped her brooch with a finger-nail. "This Mr. Severidge—is he a friend?"

"At the club. No more. We have dined once."

"What kind of a man is he?"

"Immensely able."

"But what kind," she persisted with a charming petulance, as though she were teaching a child its alphabet, "good or bad?"

"That, after all——"

"Dear me," she said, "I know it is a matter of opinion! I am asking yours. On this side of the Tweed we still distinguish between good and evil. Not by conduct only. You are too Anglo-Saxon. Which is this man: good or bad?"

Henry—or the Celtic streak in him—had known that, if he refused to answer, the conversation would end; this Highlander would retire for ever into her mountains. Nevertheless, he was not given to moral judgments, he had nothing in particular against Severidge, and, when the word "bad" appeared in his mind, it astonished him, and he could not speak it.

"Bad? As long as you know it," Mrs. Gorsand answered calmly as if the word had been spoken.

"Why should you think that?"

She took from her bag the letter Severidge had written to her in his own hand. "I do not think it," she said quietly. "I know it."

"I'm not sure that I understand."

She looked into his eyes. "No," she said, "I believe that you do not. There are things that you English have lost the faculty of understanding. You look too much; you see too little. You think it is enough to keep your eyes open; you should shut them sometimes—not only with your eyelids. A cat is blind that cannot see in the dark. It is true of nations; it is very true of the soul." Then she had taken off her brooch and held it in her hands, rolling it from one palm to the other. "So it would be of value to you to satisfy this man?"

"Yes," Henry had said.

"You are in trouble."

"Yes," he answered, though she had not asked a question.

"Then I will sell at the last price we spoke of yesterday," she said, and added at once: "There are two conditions. Mr. Severidge must come himself to fetch the manuscript. I wish to see the writer of this letter: Mr. Foolish Wiseman!"

"That ought not be difficult."

She nodded. "Second: you will come here yourself and bring your wife—what is her name?"

"Vivien."

"She has another name?"

"Vivien Mary."

"You will come on February the eighth."

Why February? why the eighth? he would have asked, but abstained. She smiled at his abstention. "You must learn history. Indeed, there are many things you must learn," she said.

"I don't doubt it," Henry answered. "I'm making a good beginning now."

"So be it," she said with a roguish glint that carried her back sixty years. "You will come, then, on that day."

He had been on the point of consenting when the jeopardy in which he stood had reappeared to him, and he answered: "I can't promise that. I would willingly. I just can't."

"You can," she said.

"I mean," he explained in hot embarrassment, "it may be

[85]

physically impossible—I mean, I can't be sure where at that time——"

"You can," she said. "I can take your promise. I do take it."

From his office on Monday morning Henry reported by telephone that the Cennini had been bought inside the price-limit.

"But you personally must fetch it."

" 'Must'?" Severidge echoed. "Why?"

"It is a condition."

"You agreed to that?"

"I did. You yourself said you would go to Glasgow."

"That may be, but I don't like dictation."

Henry put his hand over the telephone's mouthpiece. "To hell," he said to his typist's astonishment, "take it or leave it." Then he uncovered the mouthpiece. "I think," he said, "we shall have to humour the old lady."

Of the second condition he said nothing, nor did it dwell in his mind. At the end of his engagement-book he had written: "Go to Glasgow, February 8, 1935," but he had written this with a pen that Mrs. Gorsand had put before him, and now, in London, she seemed far away. Fortune pressed him hard. There was a letter from Bright's executors, and two, frightened and urgent, from his mother; his guarantee was being called. There was a letter of alarming brevity from his bank who would "be obliged if, in the extremely serious circumstances, he would make it convenient to call, when perhaps some adjustment might be reached". This letter bore Thursday's date; it had been long enough outstanding. He made an appointment by telephone and kept it that afternoon. It was at once made clear by the bleak courtesy with which he was received that the branch-manager was no longer exercising his own discretion. He had received orders from above against which no words could prevail. "We can leave it open," he said, "until Friday morning." Henry thanked him, shook hands, and returned to his office. Two clients, who intended divorce, had come to discuss the re-making of their wills. When they were gone, Henry did what throughout the day he had postponed: a triangular telephone conversation with Humphrey Waynford and his brokers arranged a meeting in the City next morning at eleven. He went home with the clear knowledge that bankruptcy proceedings were now inevitable. The rest would follow.

Vivien told him that a prospective buyer had been to see the Red House. He answered only: "Things are moving too fast." Then, while he told Vivien of Mrs. Gorsand, a shaft of thought set him smiling; he took his engagement-book from his waistcoat pocket and held it out, open at the last page.

"Look at that."

Vivien shook her head. "What of it?"

"If I am to be in Glasgow on February the eighth, it looks like a short sentence."

"Or none at all," Vivien said. "Perhaps Mrs. Gorsand has second sight. . . . Henry, seriously, I haven't given up hope."

"Haven't you?"

During the night she said: "Henry, even if I can't touch the capital of my settlement or pledge it for a loan, can't I borrow on the income? . . . I suppose terribly little in any case."

"Anyhow," he said, "you're not to do it. It may be—it probably will be—all you have to live on."

"Good heavens, can't I work?"

"Still, you are not to touch your settlement."

"That's for me to decide."

"No," he said, "it isn't. . . . Vivien, stop thinking. It's no good. Go to sleep."

She cried out angrily and sat up in the darkness. Then laughed and said: "Henry, we are quarrelling. What about? The moon?" He drew away the arm on which she was supporting herself; she came down beside him, and soon was asleep.

Next morning he went through his correspondence at his office and was in the City by eleven. Discussion was short; the securities in which the Waynford cash was to be invested were chosen and the buying-order was given. It was farcical to let the buying go forward. Better tell them now, Henry thought. But no one reaches for the noose, and he was silent. He noticed that a button on his cuff was chipped, and for each day before account-day he pressed a finger against the mound of his thumb.

Soon after three Vivien came by train to Charing Cross. She turned down Villiers Street and walked by the river to the Temple. Before turning in from the Embankment, she stood, with the trams swinging past behind her, to gaze at the river and to think: now, no one knows; therefore, nothing has happened; soon, everyone will know; but, stifled by the gross indifference of cities, she thought again that no one would notice or care; three lines at the foot of a column would record the conviction of "Henry Darrell Lerrick (29), solicitor, of Old Square, Lincoln's Inn and Hadscombe, Surrey," and she would eat the food that Kingsley brought her. She would go to bed. It would be Henry's first night in his cell. She looked at a tug plodding up-river with its string of barges, and thought: Why do we wait here? Why don't we run away?

In Gasky's chambers, her first words were: "Why does Mrs. Clutterbuck never buy you any flowers?" After this she stood at the window and asked: "If we went now, Gasky, they couldn't get us back again, could they?"

"Where? It depends on the country. . . . Anyhow, you can't do that."

Her mind was drifting like a leaf in the wind: "I suppose not. . . . Why not?"

"It's no life in any case."

"We should be together."

Even he for a moment considered it. "No," he said at last. "You can't grow old that way. Better the other. . . . Besides, it may not come to that."

They went over the familiar ground—her own settlement, the Judge's realizable securities. Vivien turned away from the barren figures. They did not add up to twenty-three thousand pounds. The telephone rang. As soon as she understood that Henry was speaking she took the receiver from the Judge's hand.

"Listen, my darling. I'm here—here in the Temple. I'll come to your office. You can drive me home?"

"Would you rather stay in London to eat?"

"No," she said. "I shall be in your office in a quarter of an hour. Good-bye."

Only when she turned back to the Judge did she understand fully that there was no way out. Until then she had always, within herself, clung to an unreasoning hope. Now she had none. She was dry and desperate. She would not let the Judge come with her and began to walk alone down flight after flight of wooden stairs. In the street she hailed a taxi. As it drew up, she saw what she must do. She gave Severidge's number in South Street. This was Tuesday night. A week ago they had dined there. He would lend the money. He would lend it at once, without question, without haggling. Without price. If she had asked him when they were together on the Bastion, he would have gone into the house for his cheque-book.

Now she pressed her body into the corner of the taxi and shut her eyes. Then, with the violent movement of sudden waking, she leaned forward and slid back the driver's window.

"Not South Street," she said. "Old Square."

"What number in Old Square?"

She told him, and, having opened the bag on her knee, took out a mirror and looked at herself with curiosity before beginning to redden her lips.

16

A BEAUTIFUL staircase curls up within a great barrel of wall from the lounge at Rodd's, partly roofing in a semicircle of armchairs and settees. This area is little used by day, for it is without a window, but in the evening, when its electric sconces and picture-lights are burning, it has an inviting intimacy.

It is nicknamed "The Kennel". Sometimes one or two members, who wish to be alone, sit there with mutual disregard; sometimes a little group assembles, and conversation—to be distinguished from chatter—grows among them; and new members learn, as part of their house-training, not to convert the Kennel into a nursery.

In any case, when Gaskony was in the club, no one took his place on the settee, under the portrait of Charles James Fox. As you came out from dinner, you glanced in that direction and, if he was there, estimated his mood. "Gaskony's in the Kennel" implied that he was alert and approachable; carrying in your glass of port, you might expect to find him in good form and look forward to a lively evening. "The Judge has gone to ground to-night" implied, on the contrary, that puppies with wagging tails would do well to keep their distance.

The evening on which Henry had informed him by telephone, before Vivien took away the receiver, that the Waynford brokers had been ordered to buy, found the Judge, to all seeing eyes, evidently gone to ground. He was not even shamming behind the newspaper which, for the sake of good talk, it was his custom so readily to lay aside. He had been silent at dinner, had gone out early, and was hunched up under the genial portrait of Fox, his right knee clasped, his head down, his eyes unregarding. "The Judge is in his lair" said the observant, and passed on. But Alan Romney, who had just been elected to a Fellowship of All Souls and had been celebrating the event with Rupert Hazell, an ensign of the Coldstream, was not on this occasion observant. Bearing with him his pink and cheerful guest, he advanced across the lounge with unwary lightness of heart. Indeed, not until he was established in the Kennel did he notice the Judge. It had by then become more discourteous to withdraw than to stay, and he said: "Good evening, Judge."

"Ah, yes," said Gaskony, coming up on the end of a long line, "good evening to 'ee."

Romney asked himself whether he should introduce his guest and so invite general conversation. In the Kennel, this was customary, but by now he had become observant and forbore. He addressed his tactful energy to the task of gently diverting Hazell's conversation to the subject of painting, which at dinner he had eagerly defended as the greatest of the arts, and away from that of certain high military officers whose behaviour provoked him to caricature and, now and then, to deep and gurgling laughter, like the noise of water poured from a bottle. It was, in a crowd, charming laughter, but was clearly undesirable within range of the Judge in his present mood, and Romney nursed his guest as anxiously as a mother nurses a baby that she has rashly brought to church.

For a time the nursing was successful. Dangerous hilarity was avoided until by chance Hazell, in the midst of grave argument, produced a saying of Leonardo's which seemed to him so apt and unanswerable that a laugh of triumph welled up in him and flowed joyfully out.

"Your guest, Romney," the Judge remarked suddenly, "has, if I may say so, a most contagious laugh."

Hazell was introduced. "I'm sorry, sir," he said. " 'Fraid I haven't got it under control."

"Not at all, sir. Not at all," the Judge replied. "I confess I began the evening blackish. I'd have sworn that laughter was a lost art until you taught me better. . . . But I think that you and Leonardo have a bad case. Come: defend it."

"Well, sir," Hazell began diffidently, "it seems to me that—" but his defence gathered ardour as it continued; Gaskony prompted him with questions; Romney's periodical summing-up gathered the threads; and other members—Floyd, a young admiral whose white tie declared him to be on his way to a party; Geoffrey Cobble with the long stiff shirt-cuffs, the tie-pin and the flowing handkerchief which where a memorial to his Edwardian elegance; and old Tripp, the schoolmaster, seeing that the Kennel had come to life, drifted in. Others followed. Well, thought the Judge, let's see what these young men are made of, and he threw up the ensign at the admiral; he appealed to Cobble as an arbiter of the niceties, thereby provoking Tripp to judgments as searching and gallantly inconsistent as Landor's; he deferred to Romney's scholarship; and, whenever the conversation showed a tendency to split into groups, he drew it together and refreshed it with a discourse of his own.

They debated the peril of discussing one art in terms of another. How far could one follow any metaphor without being misled by it? What was the effect on thought of the habit of personalizing ideas and things—of calling a ship "she" or of endowing the gods with human attributes?

"And there's another question," Romney said. "We personalize nations. We speak of England as 'she'. Is that a confusion of political thought or an elucidation of it?"

To everyone's surprise, the young Coldstreamer cut in with: "I don't see how you can love your country if you think in any other terms," and coloured when he had said it.

"Don't you?" said Geoffrey Cobble. "You can love your native village without calling it 'she'. Why not your country?"

"Because——" Hazell began, and hesitated.

"Shakespeare," said Cobble triumphantly, "doesn't agree with you. He says: 'Nought shall make us rue, if England to *itself* do rest but true'."

"But that," said the Judge, coming with a smile to Hazell's rescue, "is spoken by the Bastard, if I remember rightly. You mustn't quote him as an authority!"

The laugh that followed angered Cobble. He was an ardent Shakespearian and would not have his subject treated lightly.

The name of England led him to King Henry the Fifth whom he attacked as a boaster and a chauvinist.

"I don't agree," said Hazell. "What King Henry says seems to me to make sense all right."

"Does it?" said Cobble. "I wonder. Even in this year of grace, twenty years after the last war, are you young soldiers still spoiling for another?"

The colour deepened in Hazell's cheeks, but he controlled himself and withdrew politely into his chair.

"King Henry, as I recollect," said the Judge, "made a re-mark which——"

"He made a great many," Cobble retorted, "which in a civilized world we do well to forget."

"He made one which in a savage world we do well to re-member: 'O God of battles, steel my soldiers' hearts'."

"I have always thought," said Severidge, "that Agincourt was a gambler's battle. He ought not, in reason, to have won it."

"Steady, steady, steady!" cried Major Lenningham, "that is highly disputable on the facts," and he began to rehearse the facts, but no one took the least notice of him. Eyes were turned on Severidge. Though his words were casual, there was in their tone an element of attack, as though he were seeing King Henry and hating him. His lips were dry and he wetted them con-tinually.

"It's quite clear," he continued, "that if, before the battle, Henry had given his reasons for believing that he would win it he could have convinced no one but himself. His own con-viction can have been no more than a gambler's hunch. That's why I have no use for the man. Causes produce effects in a reasoned sequence; but just because the gamble came off, you make him a hero, and you call the battle a miracle. The con-sequence is that, following his example, other fools take like risks; they dig their heels in and call it 'faith'; and, when their gamble doesn't come off, we all pay. The truth is that what is praised as heroic faith all springs from the world's insane love of getting something for nothing—cheap victory, cheap salva-tion, results without cause: goods that aren't paid for. To say that everything has its price is to be told that you're a cynic;

but it's true. I grant you there appear to be exceptions—Agincourt was one—but the rule is that everything has to be bought at its full price."

"And would you add," old Tripp asked, "that everything can be?"

"Everything that isn't an illusion. . . . And yet, I don't know. Only the other evening the Judge proved me wrong. We were talking of Shylock's turquoise ring which he said he wouldn't have parted with for 'a wilderness of monkeys.' Well, the Judge has a book, *Marius* in two volumes,—but this is your story, Gaskony. The laugh's against me."

"You are welcome to it," the Judge said, "if it entertains you."

Severidge was surprised by this asperity. "Am I not to tell the story?"

The Judge, who had not taken his eyes from him since he and Lenningham had so suddenly appeared in the Kennel, now turned away with sick weariness, and Severidge exclaimed: "He's too modest to tell it himself. The book's of no material value. He gave eight-and-six for it long ago. But I heard him tell his brother that for reasons of his own, purely personal reasons," Severidge added with considerate discreetness, "he valued it above all his other possessions. He wouldn't part with it at any price—at *any* price. Well," he continued, pursing his lips, "people say that kind of thing without meaning it. It conflicts with my theory of reasonable cause and effect. I like to call their bluff. I tried to call the Judge's. . . . And he wasn't bluffing."

There was a laugh at this. Severidge joined in it, advanced and patted the Judge's shoulder. "Were you, Judge?"

"But, after all," said Geoffrey Cobble, "it stands to reason—unless the thing is dishonourable, of course—there must be *a* price."

"What is 'dishonourable'?" Romney asked.

Cobble turned on him. "You and your Socratic hair-splitting! Your guest would say 'selling your country', for example. And he'd be quite right. We all know what the word 'dishonourable' means, even if——"

"We all know," Romney interrupted, "but all differently."

Cobble clicked his tongue. "Anyhow, the Judge wasn't being asked to sell his country or anything else—of that kind. He was being asked to sell a book, and a book has a price. A house may be devilish tall, but every house has a roof that isn't a ruin."

"All I can say," Severidge put in, "is that if the Judge's house has a roof, I didn't reach it." Gaskony moved his lips. "I offered him twenty-five pounds. I offered him two-fifty."

The group closed in on the portrait of Charles James Fox.

"Two-fifty!"

"Was it a firm offer?"

"Oh yes, it was firm. . . . But we are annoying the Judge. It was only my game. Let's drop it." Severidge swung round on his heel.

"Does it stand?" Cobble asked.

"Oh yes," Severidge replied, "it stands." He turned back and stood facing the Judge, his feet apart, his hands in his jacket-pockets, his body inclined forward, his eyes alight. "In fact, I repeat it now—and put it up two-fifty."

"Making five hundred," said a voice.

"Five hundred?" said another.

"Well, Judge?" said a third.

Gaskony heaved his body as if to rise, but sank back. "I have nothing to say."

"A thousand," said Severidge, and, after a silence: "You see? It's his turquoise. . . . Judge, fifteen hundred."

Hazell's fingers closed on Romney's arm: "Let's clear out. I hate this. It's like bear-baiting."

"Two thousand," said Severidge. Receiving no answer, he shrugged his shoulders. "Not for a wilderness of monkeys! . . . Two thousand five." He laughed and sat down at a side-table. "I'm beat! But I'll put it in the wager-book. The Judge can sign or not. 'I wager so-and-so to a shilling that the Judge will *not* send me his *Marius* within seven days from to-day midnight. . . .' If he does send it, I pay. . . . Does that make sense?"

With the solemnity peculiar to men gambling, they began

to discuss the formula. Meanwhile Severidge wrote it, laid down the pen, stretched himself and rose. "Would you ring the bell? After that I'm thirsty."

They moved towards the wager-book. Hazell, who had been at Severidge's elbow as he wrote, was the first to read it.

"My God!" he exclaimed in a voice thickened by shock. Then quickly, in an undertone: "Alan, look at that." Then loudly and urgently to Severidge: "I say, sir, there's a mistake. You've added a nought."

"No," said Severidge.

"But you have; you have written twenty-five thousand. Three noughts. Twenty-five thousand pounds. In figures."

There was a little pause. If Severidge was surprised, he kept a gallant control.

"Only in figures?" he said. "Would you be kind and give me the book? I'll add it in words."

He wrote with a fountain-pen, then slid the book, open, with the fountain-pen in it, along the settee towards the Judge.

"But that was a slip, Severidge," Cobble cried in a shrill excited tone. "Take it back. He can't sign that! . . . You can't sign that, Gaskony."

"I mean it," said Severidge.

"He meant it," the Judge repeated. "Twenty-three thousand——"

"Twenty-five!" said three voices almost together. The third, a trifle late, was an echoing "fi-ive!"

The Judge did not hear. "I must sign that," he said, gathering the book towards him. "I *must* sign," and he signed, and breathed deeply, and rose, and began to move out. A young waiter, who had answered the bell, stood aside, with polite indifference, to let a member pass, but, seeing the face above him, gazed, forgetting all else while the old man went by, rocking as though he walked against a wind. He made his way across the lounge and through the swing-doors. The group in the Kennel moved their feet. The young waiter swallowed, and asked which gentleman had rung.

17

Outside the club there was a warm drizzle of rain. The Judge lifted his face to it and held out his hands, then crossed the road and turned into Pall Mall.

The scene from which he had come left a stain upon him, as though it were a brawl from which he had escaped. The movement of his thought was clogged by a sick disgust, welling up, like some viscous fluid, from an evil dream. What he must do, he knew clearly. While Cobble was twittering "You can't sign, you can't sign," he had known—or rather, had seen, for the resolve had been instantaneous like a burst of light—that he must tie up a book in paper and string, and send it. Even now, as his feet moved on the glistening pavement, the process of his mind was visual, not rational. He saw his difficulty in finding paper and string—on the dresser? in the card-board box?— and fumbled in the empty kitchen, where the tap dripped under a bare electric bulb. He saw, too, the lettering on the spine of the books and read: *Marius the Epicurean*. No pang of regret; no recognition; resolve, a needle thrust home suddenly, had anaesthetized an area of thought.

By the time he reached the Temple he was exhausted, but he said to the porter at the outer gate: "I shall be troubling you again. I have a packet for the night-post."

"Shall I send it out for you, Master? I've a pal here going out presently."

"Thank'ee. Thank'ee, no. I'll take it."

Up the wooden stairs. The private bookshelf: *Marius the Epicurean*. Brown paper—easy. String—in the saucer, tied up in loops. . . . Fold in the edges, hold, tie. . . . Too fast. . . .

He sat down, listening to the tap. . . . Pall Mall. Rodd's. All those faces. . . . Fold in the edge, hold, tie. . . . He made for the door. But he must first address his parcel with a pen in the living-room, where the clock—the clock seemed to have stopped, and yet, when he looked in through the glass panel, the pendulum was moving silently within; and he wrote, in a rectangle of string: George Severidge, Esq. Nothing in his memory would give him the number in South Street, and he sat watching the pendulum until his hand touched the telephone-book. Small print, he couldn't see, but, when he carried the book to the bare light over the sink, he could see, and wrote in the address with a scratchy pen of Mrs. Clutterbuck's. Why were the necks of cheap ink-bottles always too small for the pen. Pen inky. Finger inky. He sucked it. No matter. . . . Now . . .

The wooden stairs; the porter. Up Fleet Street a solitary bus was taking the compositors home. In the all-night post-office his parcel slid away down a chute.

"Good-night."

"Good-night, sir."

Fleet Street again. The porter.

"Good-night, Master."

"Good-night to 'ee."

The first flight of wooden stairs, the second, the third. Why was the door of his flat open? Why were the lights on? Who's there? Who's there? No one.

Next morning Mrs. Clutterbuck found him hard to wake. She stood beside him until he sat up in his blue-striped pyjamas and began to drink his morning tea. He had been late last night, he said; he had had to take out a parcel. "All the kitchen lights was on," said Mrs. Clutterbuck, "and the hall lights too."

The fiery numbness of the previous night was gone. His thought ran hither and thither, picking out the truth, as it had been accustomed to pick out from a mass of evidence those indications, conflicting or according, which might be pieced together into a summing-up. It just shows you, he thought, how little a crowd knows, how dangerous even honest witnesses are for the most part; they see and hear, but they are utterly shut out from the feeling of a thing; if Tripp and Floyd had known what was happening, if little Cobble even had had a notion of it, it wouldn't have happened; they'd have seen it ugly, bad taste, what you will, and it couldn't have happened. As it was—well, Romney was uneasy, that guest of his too, as some men are said to be when there's a cat in the room, but they didn't know why—and they won't ever know.

He got up, shaved and went to his bath. This was Wednesday. Severidge would pay on the nail. He'd wait for that; he would say nothing to Henry until the money was in hand; and Henry and I, he thought, will have to concoct for Vivien some story of where the money came from—any technical jargon will do, women don't listen about money; if they have been brought up in a steady flow of it, how it comes is all Greek to them—dull Greek, too: tell them about the creation of a sinking-fund, show them a company's balance-sheet or a trust-account, and they try to listen at first, but it's no good—in their hearts they don't believe in it, they think it's all hokum, and perhaps it is. . . . Think of a balance-sheet after a hundred years!—whereas the domestic accounts of a Stuart household still tell you what men ate, what they wore, what pleasures they valued, how they lived. . . . Anyhow, Vivien, he decided, is not to know that the money was the price of *Marius*. Severidge won't tell her for his credit's sake.

While he was dressing, he perceived, with enough shock to delay his hand reaching for his hair-brush, that the fantasy of the whole transaction would not explain itself to the men at Rodd's as it explained itself to him. They, or some of them would think, or half-think, that Severidge had not meant to write £25,000—that only his pride had backed his error, once made. Believing that, they'd believe also that the wager ought not to have been taken up and that he, Gaskony, had been— well, mighty quick to seize his advantage. The riddle of the "extra nought" would be long debated, some saying that Severidge, if he had enough ill-taste to burn his money in public, deserved to be caught, but adding, nevertheless, with a shrug, that it would have been better if the Judge hadn't signed or, having signed, had kept his book and paid his shilling.

Even now, when the book was gone, the Judge felt himself touched by the fierce, stubborn pride he would have had in refusing to sign. But he saw it now, as he had suddenly seen it in the moment of decision, as pride in defence of an unreality. While Severidge had baited and taunted him, he had been shaken by nothing but the white emotion of his resolve not to sell, a defiant rage; but when the pack was whining "twenty-five, twenty-fi-ive!" he had seen that he himself had been wrong. His clinging to the dead book was wrong, not only in relation to the demand of Vivien's life, but wrong absolutely, a false pride of the spirit, a lust for delusion in the same category with Severidge's own. His *Marius* had, in the instant, ceased to be Julia's *Marius*, had become simply a book that he must pack and send—not his integrity as he had so passionately, so arrogantly believed, but a false symbol of which to disburden his life. No pang of regret, no sense of defeat or self-betrayal now touched him—only a knowledge of freedom such as comes rarely to men when their youth is over, a feeling, at once glorious and tentative, of having outgrown a delusion, of having learned something and of having more to learn.

The sun was shining as he drove to Rodd's. There, almost certainly, at luncheon or after it, he would find Severidge. The story will have spread, Gaskony thought; he'll come to bask in the glow of it—to play sphinx before the enigma of the extra nought. He found Severidge there before him, perched on the lounge-fender, the centre of a group, and he said:

"Well, you've won."

"What do you mean—I've won?"

"I have sent the book."

A strange expression, which the Judge had seen only once before, now passed over Severidge's face—the same expression of triumph and thwartedness, of exaltation and sagging, which had appeared in the wide-open eyes of a prisoner while a witness described how he had found the body of a woman whom that prisoner had debauched and killed. Such longing! Such disappointment! Such heaven, such hell! So great a weariness and dryness! Such unappeasable thirst! Watching the prisoner, and Severidge now, Gaskony's mind reflected the most terrible of sonnets—

> Enjoy'd no sooner but despisèd straight:
> Past reason hunted; and no sooner had,
> Past reason hated, as a swallowed bait—

and he pulled his hand across his eyes, as he had long ago in Court.

"It hasn't come," Severidge answered.

"I posted it last night. It will."

Severidge could smile now, as the prisoner had. There are lusts of the spirit as of the flesh.

> Mad in pursuit, and in possession so;
> Had, having, and in quest to have, extreme;
> A bliss in proof, and proved, a very woe,

but the lusts of the spirit, too, have their pride, their swagger, and Severidge said quietly:

"I take your word for it. I'm going to Glasgow. I may go on to Edinburgh. I'll give you a cheque now."

He wrote it on his knee. The hand of another conveyed and the Judge took it. In the thought of those who watched, he was, he knew, "selling out"; he felt their silence but was beyond its influence. The cheque was drawn on his own bank in St. James's. After lunch he paid it in, and, as he carried no cheque-book, asked for a loose cheque. With this he went to Henry's office. He had to wait; Henry had a client with him; and, while waiting, he filled in the loose cheque for twenty-three thousand pounds. Twenty-three? Twenty-five? Twenty-three was the urgent need. The rest could follow.

Soon he was taken into Henry's room and gave the cheque to him. He wished to avoid gratitude; he wished to avoid

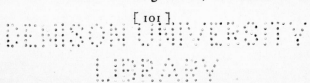
DENISON UNIVERSITY
LIBRARY
GRANVILLE OHIO

explanation. He was tired and sat down astride an upright chair.

"Never mind how. . . . In fact, from Severidge. . . . You'll be told how when next you go to Rodd's. But don't forget, you have no knowledge of it until you are told."

But Henry renewed his questions.

"I sold my *Marius,*" the Judge said.

"But not for *this!*"

"For more. Twenty-five."

"For *Marius!*"

"Oh, he was bidding for more than that."

Henry asked no more, accepting with a long sigh, almost a groan, what the gods, as yet inexplicably, had given. He moved his hand to the telephone. "I'll tell Vivien—or will you?"

The Judge stayed the outstretched hand. "Not now. Tell her when you have had time to think. . . . She's not to know how this money came."

"Not know?"

"Never."

"But what am I to say?"

"Say that I was able after all to borrow it at interest. She won't ask on what security. If she should—oh, for God's sake, boy, use your brains. Talk jargon. She's not a banker."

He rose and shifted to a more comfortable chair. "Now give me tea. We'll talk about it." Then, looking at Henry's white face, he said in a tone of surprise: "Well, we are out of the wood."

DENISON UNIVERSITY
LIBRARY
GRANVILLE, OHIO

18

FIVE days passed. Henry met his obligations and—mark of firm intention now—pressed on towards a probable sale of the Red House. Gaskony celebrated their being "out of the wood" by taking Vivien in a steam-boat up the river from Richmond to Windsor. They dined at Windsor and came into London by car. He was content in her serene company. The days of tension had fallen away into the past—by consent unspoken of; and, when he was alone again in the Temple, the sun of that long, quiet day still glowed in him, the flow of water and the chugging paddles sounded in his ears. He put on an old dressing-gown and settled to his *Athenian* files.

The next night, at the oval table at Rodd's, Severidge, having just taken his place there, leaned forward and said:

"What is it, Judge—a joke?"

"Is what a joke?"

"I came back from Scotland this morning. . . . No book." Gaskony was silent, not yet understanding, and Severidge continued: "No book has arrived."

"It must have arrived long ago."

Severidge broke into a laugh: "Good God! You don't mean seriously that you did sénd it?"

"Certainly I did."

"I was prepared to laugh at—well, at what seemed to me a poor joke," Severidge said. "As it is——"

"I posted it that same night at the all-night post-office in Fleet Street."

"Registered?"

"No."

Eyebrows went up, and the Judge saw that the oval table thought him wrong. Perhaps he had been, this being the modern world; but he had been following custom. In the past, there had been things you registered and things you didn't.

"No," he said, " I didn't register it. My rule is to register valuables—jewels, keys, documents. Not books."

Severidge smiled. "A very Victorian habit."

"Very," said the Judge. "None the worse for that. This is London, not Timbuctoo. . . . But the post-office will remember my going in. The porter at the gate of the Temple——"

"My dear Gaskony, if you say you posted it, your word of course is enough."

The Judge saw clearly that he was trapped and he opened his lips with the intention of saying that, if the book were not found, the wager should be off; he would return the money. How easy it might have been to say that!—so easy that almost he said it without thinking. How easy Severidge, waiting for his money, supposed the return of it to be! Wasn't it snug in the bank waiting to be retransferred from one account to the other? The Judge hesitated, seeing how much deeper the trap was than Severidge knew—or shall ever know, he thought, or shall ever know! And he said aloud: "Evidently, if the book doesn't turn up, the wager is off. Your stake will come back to you."

The members within earshot murmured their approval. An old general roused himself from his fish to say: "best thing that could have happened. Call it off. Never liked it." He smiled affably and sipped his wine. "Can say so now. Never liked it. Stakes too high. High stakes make bad blood."

Out of a momentary silence, and with a nervous twitch of the face as if he were making a joke of which he was uncertain, Severidge looked up and said: "Anyhow, if my stake does come back, it comes back less eight and sixpence." No one saw the point of this. "That makes it fair. That puts the account straight." Still no one saw the point, but they all nodded as if they did.

19

SEVERIDGE, having paid in Glasgow for Cennini's *Treatise* more than it cost him in money, had come out of Mrs. Gorsand's presence sick at heart, and gone on at once to Edinburgh where he had business. On the way home he had remembered that Gaskony's *Marius* would be at South Street. The book, the material thing, was valueless to him. That in obtaining it he had pricked the balloon of the Judge's integrity gave him, in retrospect, the same pleasure, the same ache of unfulfilment and nothingness, that he had in recalling his sterile captures of women who, captured, were but bodies and names.

His judgment was fretted by two vexations: that men would think him a fool for having bid so much; that they would nevertheless doubt always whether he had originally intended to write in figures "£25,000". He valued his reputation for infallible self-control, for moving within an unshrinking margin of discretion, for carrying "soundness" to the point of genius, for being hard, a realist, successfully calculating, imperturbably cool; so extravagant a bid as he had made conflicted with this reputation; it would be thought "queer". He valued, too, a different image of himself as a Regency buck. To be free of the card-room at Rodd's was his compensation for not being a man of family; he played cards nowhere else, and played there always in mental fancy-dress; and he had long ago determined, when he saw guests reverently examining the brown and angular handwriting of the old wager-books, to write history there. He had written it; and the fools would smile as they turned his page and say: "Here's the merchant who wrote an extra nought by mistake. . . . By mistake? . . .

So the story goes." He heard the silly lie twittering down the years as little Goeffrey Cobble had twittered it that night. "You were wrong, my dear Cobble. You are doing Gaskony an injustice. I wrote those figures deliberately." But Cobble hadn't believed it. "Well, anyhow," he had said, "decent of you to stick to it."

Arrived at South Street, Severidge had found *Marius* among a heap of parcels and correspondence unopened by his secretary because it was his rule that she should open only what was typewritten. Suddenly he had seen how it was possible, by pretending not to have received the book, both to preserve his satisfaction in the Judge's surrender and, in effect, to call the wager off. The ingenuity of the idea caused it to present itself to him as an adroit practical joke. Stealing? Nonsense, no money would pass, or, rather, the money, his own, would re-pass. But the Judge would lose his book. Impossible to return it. This nibbled at Severidge's conscience. He saw it as a theft of the book's cost.

Therefore, at dinner that night, he had spoken as he did. He would accept, not twenty-five thousand pounds but twenty-five thousand less eight-and-six. "That makes it fair. That puts the account straight." For him this was true. It was a joke and not a joke. To others, he knew, it would seem niggling or meaningless; it had needed courage in him to say it. Nevertheless to say it had been necessary; it was a part of his accuracy, it untied a knot in his mind.

20

"Your stake will come back to you," Gaskony had said. How, he had not known; but his voice had said it without misgiving as though, within him, there were a strength that would enable him to walk on those troubled waters. Soon afterwards common sense and calculation beset him again, misgivings returned, and he began to sink.

In the club that evening, until he could endure it no longer, and afterwards in the Temple, he cast himself back upon his list of investments, which by now he knew almost by heart, and found no help there. The figures were barren, but they clung to him like burrs. If he had been unable to raise twenty-three thousand pounds when Henry needed it, how could he raise it now? To pay, he would have to sell every security he possessed and commute his pension as well. His personal belongings would have to go. Nothing would remain to live on; he would be poorer than Mrs. Clutterbuck; even so there might not be enough.

How much would there be? He thought of it in terms of his own death. If he died and no provision had to be made for his maintenance—the grave having at any rate that merit—how much would he cut up for? Call it, whatever it was, his Death Value. As in fact he wasn't dying, add to it the amount he would get by commuting his pension. What would the total be? Twenty-three thousand? Possibly. It depended on what lump-sum he could get for his pension. Not much. He was hale and hearty, what an insurance company would call "a good life", but still—sixty-six. Not much would he get, but a few thousands—enough, perhaps, to make the difference.

Then there were his personal effects, watch and chain, pearl studs, furniture, cuff-links, clock, ivory brushes, those bronzes, this armchair—they'd fetch a bit. He had inventories of them. Add it all together—Death Value plus commuted pension; it might just foot the bill.

He stood up and began to walk to and fro, four short paces, between chair and window. What was the good of thinking in those terms? He wasn't dead by a long chalk; he had to live; and he looked at the comfortable room, thinking—as he had when Henry had sat there with his troubles and Vivien with hers—of course, this can go; I can cut down; still, there must be something left; one has to be reasonable. At this his mind halted and, as it were, blinked astonishment at the place to which it was come.

Not until now had he contemplated the surrender of his pension. Or had he? While Henry was adding up figures, had he not vaguely wondered what the capitalized value of his pension would be? The notion had slipped away from him—or he had put it away—and he had thought thenceforward only of the stock he might sell, reserving his pension to himself as his own last ditch. And now he had been counting it up as an asset possibly to be surrendered. . . . To pay off Severidge, yes. . . . To get myself out of a scrape, yes. . . . To keep Vivien's husband out of prison, no. . . . Good God! that's how my mind works! Queer. "Know thyself," said the Greeks. I'm beginning to learn. Selfishness?—but that was deliberate. This had been worse. By habit, conventionality, plain blindness, the idea of forfeiting his pension had, until now, been shut out of his mind.

Even so, even if by this means he could pay off Severidge, how was he to live? Not by borrowing. He had faced that possibility and rejected it when the trouble was Henry's, and rejected it as firmly now. He could, he supposed, earn a few guineas with his pen, but chiefly in the learned quarterlies, and precious few guineas they would yield. Besides, if he were to set up as a hack journalist at his time of life, what would become of his *Athenian?* What would become of his *Athenian* anyway? It needed leisure and peace of mind. If he had failed to write it with comfortable means behind him, what hope was there now? . . . In any case, how was he to live? He remembered real poverty—in lodgings with Phil Brown, no money to have his boots patched, going without fuel when it was cold, cutting down food to buy *Marius*. At his age, he couldn't go back to that.

Why not? He had never been happier—but he had been happy, in those conditions, precisely because he had been young, because Phil had shared them with him and Julia had been alive. There had been a future. Now . . .

And yet—why not? Suppose he were to say to himself: my habits, my conventions, my comfortable means are what tie me down; they are what age me; they and the condition of life they represent have stood between me and my *Athenian*—suppose he were to say that? He said it, sceptically at first, and listened to it as he might have listened to a young man prattling to him of poverty and the simple life: sceptically, not with hostility; with humorous consideration, not with contempt; with a shrewd regard for the practicable—and yet, suddenly, with yearning! Is any man too old to accept, with joyful equanimity, a revolution in his life?—then he is already dead. Is he too stubborn and fearful to be reborn?—then he is a clothes-prop, a dummy of the armchair. Is he so wrapped in custom that he cannot strip and be his naked self—then, in himself, he exists no longer but is of the mass, the mob, the ugly and nameless proletariat of the soul.

Gaskony sat down on the fender and stared. A Greek epigram looked up at him: "Νυκτὸς ἀπερχομένης . . . Day by day we are born as night retires . . . beginning to-day the life that remains. Do not then call thyself, old man, abundant in years; for to-day thou hast no share in what is gone." . . . Well, he thought, that cuts both ways. It doesn't make you young again, but it gives you a fair chance not to be a coward. He pulled a time-table from its shelf and chose a morning train to Oxford.

21

THE Provost of St. Peter's was astonished by his brother's un-heralded arrival in the middle of the forenoon, but its very unexpectedness and the fact that his visitor had forgotten to take off his gloves warned him not to allow astonishment to appear. He took a dispatch-case from the Judge's hand.

"Hullo, Will, lucky I'm here. I was just going out."

"Must you?"

Though the appointment was not easy to miss, the Provost said: "By no means. . . . Have some breakfast? You can't have had time for much."

The Judge shook his head. He had seated himself on the edge of a chair. "Busy?" he inquired.

"No."

"Can I have half an hour now? . . . More later? . . . I've left a bag at the lodge. I want to stay the night."

"You can have all day—and all night if you need it. You had better begin by taking those gloves off. Then, when you feel like it, you'll be able to handle that decanter at your elbow."

The Judge looked at his gloves. "'Pon my word! What's gone wrong with me?"

The Provost surveyed him with a smile. "A bit flurried, I should say. . . . But early rising does you good. You look about twenty-five this morning, apart from the grey hairs.

"All right," said the Judge, "then you had better treat me as twenty-five. That's just what I need. . . . Look here, Dick. You are the executive one in our family. This is the point at which you take charge. Something pretty odd has happened.

I have decided—but I suppose I had better begin at the beginning."

He told the whole story.

"And what," said Dick Gaskony, "is the answer to that one?
I can lend you a bit."

"Thank'ee, no. But I think I have the answer. I want you to
check up. If it works on paper, I want you to put it into effect;
accept power of attorney, act for me." He took from his dispatch-case two thin foolscap volumes and laid them on the
desk. "List of securities. Valuation for insurance of every
stick I possess. Estimate their market-value. Add a current
balance, not counting the two thousand of Severidge's that
hasn't gone up the spout, of £489. Find out what I can get
for my pension, assuming a doctor passes me A1. Add them
together. I make them come to about enough—and a bit
over."

"How much over?"

"That's what I want you to find out."

"Enough to live on?"

"Enough for me."

Dick Gaskony took off his glasses, looked at his brother and
spoke with the severity he might have used towards an unreasoning child. "Enough to live decently?"

"No, Dick," the Judge answered with a twinkle and a slow
survey of the panelled room, "not to live in that state of life
unto which, so surprisingly, it has pleased God hitherto to call
us."

"By which you mean?"

"I mean that there may be enough to give me, on an annuity,
three pounds a week. And there may be a tiny nest-egg, perhaps
two hundred, over and above."

"And then?" Dick Gaskony replied in the tone of one who
was being asked to take a fairy-tale seriously. "What then?
You can't live on three pounds a week. A suit of clothes is a
month's income and more."

"I have lived on less."

"Not at the present cost of living."

"That's true. . . . I know, Dick. But I have my eyes open. I'm going to be poorer than I was when I was a student. But it can be done."

His plan was clear and he unfolded it with an eager lucidity. "Do you remember Vivien's nursery governess? Louisa? Lou, we called her. Left us to be married fifteen years ago. She's a widow now, Mrs. Hagg—unfortunate name, I grant you, but a good woman. She never disturbed my papers. She treated my *Athenian* as if he were the family ghost to be flattered and propitiated, which is about what he has been all these years. You said once, Dick, that, if I had married, my *Athenian* would have been looked after. Lou would have qualified in that respect, I assure you. She acquired a distant passion for what she called the dead languages. At bedtime, I used to put Vivien to sleep on the Odyssey——"

"Did you indeed?" said Dick. "What translation?"

"What translation! What do you think?" the Judge inquired indignantly. "And why not my own? . . . And the Greek, too, for the grand noise of it. All children love incantations. If only you chaps who teach——"

"Yes, Will," the Provost interrupted, "you were talking about Mrs. Hagg."

"Very well," the Judge answered. "Lou has always kept in touch. Letter on Vivien's birthday, letter at Christmas. She has a boy of thirteen, William Vivien if you please, and she encloses bits of his Latin. Not too bad either. . . . Well, since her husband's death she has kept lodgings in Cliftonville. I'm going to live with her. She'll take me and feed me and wash me for less than three pounds—fifty shillings all the year round will leave her a profit. She's empty in the winter. I shall be content with a room that her more prosperous lodgers don't hanker after."

"Cliftonville?" said the Provost. "It sounds like a scene in a musical comedy. Where is it?"

"Come, Dick! Even in Oxford such ignorance won't pass. Ever heard of Margate—popular seaside resort in the County of Kent?"

"Yes," said Dick, "Margate I know."

"Well, Cliftonville is, in effect, part of it."

"And you propose to live there?"

"I do."

"All the year round?"

"All the year round."

"Bless you, Will, you're mad." The Provost looked at his brother long and silently; then said: "No, you're not. You're sane. You're completely right. Inhumanly right. Your *Athenian* will get itself written in that lodging and nowhere else on earth."

The Judge loved his brother in that moment more than he had ever loved him. Not to doubt, not to quibble, not to be worldly wise, to know when dream is utmost reality, to accept another's revolution as one accepts his "good-morning"—this is brotherly love; and the Judge, awkwardly acknowledging it, said: "I'm glad I came here. I might not have been able to stand too much cold water."

"Well," the Provost answered, withdrawing for both their sakes, and for custom's sake, from the dangerous ground of personal sentiment, "my rule in life—being a complex fool myself, and so were you, Will, when last we met—my rule is to respect the simplicities when I meet them, which isn't often. Whom the gods wish to save they first drive mad—clean out of their complex sanities. Do you remember Nietzsche? Zimmern quotes it: 'The Greeks are like genius, simple'—*einfach* is Nietzsche's word. . . ." The Provost left his desk and went over to the window, opening and closing his hands, which were crossed behind him.

"I talk too much for the executive member of our family. What precisely do you want me to do?"

"Everything. Sell me up, lock, stock and barrel—everything except my books and my files. Pay Severidge. Negotiate the annuity. My body is at your disposal for medical inspection. I have no debts. Income-tax outstanding is provided for in a separate deposit account. It's plain sailing. When you know the figures with fair accuracy, tell me what is left over. If it's as much as two-fifty, I shall go to Athens for as long as the money lasts—until the New Year, maybe."

"Greece in winter?"

"That's why. I have never been there then."

"Pretty bleak, my dear Will."

But the Judge knew his mind. "Besides," he said, "there's good reason to go at the moment. It's where Vivien and Henry would expect me to go. It will prevent them from finding out before they need that I am in Queer Street. When I'm gone, you must talk to Henry—he will get the story at Rodd's and wonder how I raised the money. Tell him to keep quiet. In the circumstances, he'll do what I ask. It's Vivien who mustn't know that I am down and out."

"She's bound to in the end."

"That may be, that may be," said the Judge, "but not now. I don't want a scene. I don't want to explain. I want—this thing—to be my own for a bit. Do you see why?"

"Oh yes," said the Provost, "I see why. Young men feel like that when they fall in love."

The Judge received this without comment, and vigorously pursued his course. "Once I'm back," he said, "and settled at Lou's and writing, Vivien can find out the truth for herself. Then it won't make her unhappy—oughtn't to—she's not a fool. At the moment, she'd blame herself for having ruined me—or blame Henry. All the 'complex sanities'! I'm afraid of that."

"Afraid?"

"Dick, Dick, be patient with me. As far as this thing is concerned, I was born yesterday. I have to learn to walk on the waters."

The Provost accepted that. He dropped the list of securities and the valuation into a drawer. "In Athens," he asked, "do you propose to write? You can't take with you a twentieth part of your material."

"No," the Judge said. "I shall travel light."

22

HAVING visited Cliftonville and secured his retreat against the day when his money should run out in Greece, Gaskony parted without a tremor from his Temple chambers, still intact; the sale would follow his going; his eyes did not fall upon emptied shelves or the pale rectangles of pictures removed, nor did the boots of the removers shuffle, in his hearing, across bare floor-boards. He walked out on a summer's morning and had not to attend the funeral of his dead life.

To Vivien his departure was unsurprising. She had asked him a hundred times why he did not go to Greece again, and now he was gone.

A flatness, a feeling of monotony, of indefinable disappointment, had supervened upon her life when she and Henry found themselves, as the Judge had said, "out of the wood". It was as if a war had ended, a threat of invasion been lifted. She had keyed herself to endurance, had drawn courage from her deepest reserves; now nothing was required of her. The Red House was sold and they moved into a flat in Chelsea. Employment came to Henry from Severidge personally, then from C.M.I.; he worked early and late to deserve it, travelled indefatigably to the North and the Midlands—wherever C.M.I.'s interests lay, and, in what might have been his leisure, elaborated a scheme of endowment which Severidge had vaguely spoken of. "The Vanity Trust", Henry secretly called it; "The Severidge Foundation" was its nobler name. To Henry at first it was a chance for Bright, Lerrick; then, because its general purpose was to do for the liberal arts what great capital was already doing for scientific research, he became interested in it for its own sake and planned it with a crusader's devotion. In this he looked to Vivien for partnership, but she could not respond. His enthusiasm, which would in the past have delighted her, even his hard work and moderation of life which her gladness might have rewarded, struck no warmth from her. She said how glad she was, she praised him and gave him all the help she could, she saw that now at last there was offered to her that fusion of two lives which she had longed for, but she could not herself enter into it. Henry's former weakness, which she had not held against him while their common peril lasted, arose in her memory. Not his own wisdom but, as she understood, some financial manipulation of Gasky's had rescued him from it, and his invariable avoidance of any detailed discussion of Gasky's part in the matter seemed to her shamefaced. One evening he showed her a new account book he had bought. Gasky, he explained, did not consider that they were in debt to him. He had said that the money was, in effect, hers, which he would have left to her; she would be so much the poorer when he died. "All the same," said Henry, "I mean to redeem that money. First I shall pay off my mother's outstanding debt. Meanwhile interest and sinking-fund payments will have to accumulate on the wrong side of this account book; but as soon as the Bright people are paid off, every penny we save is going on to the right side of it and into a separate banking account. If Gasky dies, then the money is yours personally, which is what he would wish. When at last that's done, I shall breathe again with my head above water."

When Severidge told her that her husband was one of the ablest young men he knew, she thought how, in the past, she would have gone home eager to tell Henry, and how he and she together would have celebrated this laurel upon their young fortune. Now she could not but think how Severidge's manner would change if ever he were to know how near to prison Henry had been that evening when they had dined at South Street. She felt that she was deceiving Severidge, who spoke always with so much candour of the working of his own mind, and whenever he praised Henry, as he often did, she was embarrassed by her secrecy, which implied discredit of her marriage. It was, Severidge would tell her with smiling deference, a marriage that Don Juan would respect for its own sake—apart from the rules; and once, on the same balcony in South Street, he reminded her of how, with her hand on Henry's arm, she had intervened to say that "we" were "all-of-a-piece".

"I think," he added, "it was your saying that that first made me value you. How you two were on edge that night!"

"Yes," she answered. "I told you at Felden that we were spending too much. Now we have sold the Red House and cut down expenses. So we are out of the wood."

"And yet," he said, "you are in fact less happy than you were then."

He was so near her that she almost moved away. "Why do you say that?"

"Isn't it true?"

"Not in the least!"

He shrugged his shoulders, and, at that disclaiming shrug, she cried out like a distracted child: "Why do you do that?"

"What?"

"Shrug . . . doubt me!"

"I'm sorry. . . . Only because I'm fond of you."

She saw the conversation tip dangerously.

"Perhaps you are half-right," she said to restore its balance, "but it's only that I'm tired—not unhappy. Moving house. The summer in London. I miss the Hadscombe garden."

This commonplace was a warning that Severidge knew well how to accept. He had observed that she had not withdrawn when he came close to her; this, for the moment, was enough; he was content to hold his ground, then by retreat to let her feel at once the flattery of his desire, the honour of his discretion.

"Why don't you take a holiday before the summer is over? Take him to Scotland."

"He has too much work."

"For me?"

"Partly."

"That can be arranged."

"He will refuse to miss anything."

"Look," he said, "you will think I am trying to be rid of you. But be wise. Make him go with you."

23

HENRY would not go. This inrush of work was, he said, a tide that must be taken at the flood, and Vivien did not press him. To have conveyed that the holiday had been suggested by Severidge himself would have been to wound his self-esteem. The work he did with such unswerving devotion was, she knew well, his attempt to vindicate himself in her eyes and his own; he spoke of their "fresh start" and valued whatever was new in their flat more than anything that had survived from the Red House; he was trying to remake their life, to remake himself above all, and this with a cheerful humility and patience which she recognized as fresh woods in his love for her; but her responses were artificial; he was much absent and, instead of longing for his return, she had to prepare herself for it and to compel her interest in the little triumphs, the new plans, that he brought back to her. She loved him now, not for his part in their singleness but, as if they were separate human beings, for his goodness seen objectively; she could not escape her knowledge of the extent to which they owed to Severidge their increasing fortune—it seemed to be no longer theirs. Henry, too, was aware of their debt to Severidge, but he acknowledged it laughingly as a triumph of *theirs*, saying that she had be-witched the man and kissing her gratefully; but she had no longer his saving sense of their impregnable unity; when she had been in Severidge's company, she saw Henry, lovingly or critically, from outside their secret bond, and sometimes his eagerness presented itself to her, in contrast with Severidge's deeply-founded self-assurance, as that of an industrious ap-prentice. The more Severidge praised Henry and deferred to him as being young and, in his marriage, supremely fortunate, the more aware was she of having begun to see life with harder eyes, of having outgrown the simplicity of her former values. In a letter she wrote to Greece she said: "We are settled down in our new flat. Henry is working as never before. You were quite right about him: he was worth rescuing!" In another, she said: "We went to a play with Mr. Severidge last night. What is it about men of that kind? They make you feel as if they were somehow *exempt*. If there was a revolution or an earth-quake it wouldn't touch them. It's not that they are rich. Nowadays lots of very rich people seem like lambs for the slaughter. But S. doesn't. Henry says he has agents in every camp so that he will always come out on top, whichever side wins. That sounds easy, but you must know how to control the agents. It's not simply a question of paying them. You must have a different currency for each." And in a third letter, sent in the early autumn, she wrote: "Our voyage to Windsor together seems far away—as far as the days when you told me the story of Nausicaa. How many times did I make you tell me that story? When are you coming back? I used to think then that I *was* Nausicaa. I don't feel like her now. More like Penelope, which isn't so good. I have persuaded Henry to say that he may take a holiday at Christmas time, but I don't suppose he will. He has written to you about the partner he is taking in, Mr. Dennacre. Mr. Dennacre will be installed by Christmas so there is just a chance that we might get away. Henry is growing younger every day, but I'm not, so come back soon. Or are you going to live in Greece? Shall I take an aeroplane? But we are economizing hard. When you come back to the Temple, it will all be easier than when we were at Hadscombe. You will be within easy reach."

Before the winter hardened, she stayed three times at Felden, twice with Henry and once, in mid-November, without him. There had always been other guests. Henry, as gay as ever and more confident, had made new friends, and had discussed with her, in their bedroom, the advance they were making. "You know," he said, "we are in a fair way now to establishing a big commercial practice. Dennacre won't be enough before another year is out." But whereas, in the past, they had jointly made a new friend, now they made different friends, or the same friend by different approaches. Even Severidge, she and Henry knew differently, she having with him an intimacy of conversations remembered, of books lent and discussed, of point of view, about which Henry needed to be informed. When they three were together there was talk that excluded him without her knowing it. Long afterwards he would say, while putting on his tie: "What was he talking about in the garden—Nausicaa and all that, and you as a little girl?" and she had to explain that she had been telling Severidge about Gasky's story-telling.

During her November visit to Felden, Severidge asked her why she didn't put Henry into Parliament. He was the right age, a good mixer; his manner was first-rate and he had a quick grasp. Her answer would have been that she and Henry had always seen their life as private; the last thing they had wanted was power. But she said now:

"It's not for me to 'put' him into anything."

"That's only a way of speaking," Severidge replied. "That's neither here nor there. . . . The point is that people of your sort ought not to leave politics to the rag, tag and bobtail. You ought not to shirk power if you can see your way to it. I'll have a word with Henry. The way lies open."

To Severidge all ways lay open, and she found, as she discussed this subject with him, that her former view that political life was a vocation which you had or had not, an activity which was in harmony or in disharmony with your nature, was a view more ingenuous than she had supposed. Severidge argued that political activity was a part of one's civic duty; and when she replied that nevertheless it was not, and could not be, every man's civic duty to enter Parliament, he said no: every man hadn't the chance, but Henry had; it was a great opportunity; it opened the way to so many——

" 'Kingdoms of this world'?"

"Well," he said, "anyhow, it is the world we live in."

"I suppose it is."

Then he said: "How strange you are! No one else I know would say: 'I suppose it is!' quite like that. You cling stubbornly to the 'clouds of glory'. I suppose that means, quite simply, that you are good." He came away from the fire by which he had been standing and leaned over her sofa, his hands upon its back, his shoulders thrust up by the weight of his body thrown forward. He was looking out beyond her to the window, blurred by November's rain which beat upon it in noisy gusts. "No one has ever been able, in reason, to tell me the meaning of the word 'good'," he said. "My sister, who is a religious woman, says that most people have an intuition of its meaning, and that I haven't. So much the worse for me, I suppose. But you at least, even when I think you a fool, make me see that the word probably has a meaning."

She knew suddenly that, if she tried to move, his hand would shift to prevent her, so she lay still and said: "Do you think I'm a fool because I don't particularly want Henry to go into politics?"

But he was not to be diverted. "Yes. But I don't care whether he goes into politics or not. He has quite enough. . . . Do you remember that day early in the summer when Laurence Sarrett came over? We went to church. Afterwards my sister was angry with me on your account."

"On mine? Why?"

"I don't know. Some little thing I had done or hadn't done—I forget. That's not the point. But, as we were walking home—you and Laurence had gone on ahead—she said something I shall never forget. She said she loved me and wasn't afraid of me. She said she was the only person I know on earth of whom either of those things was true. That was pretty bleak. It was bleak then—it's much bleaker now."

She moved; he stayed her with a quick, light hand. "Yes," he said, "you fear me, I know. But you needn't. I am not even going to say that I love you." He straightened himself, left her and walked back to the fire, where he stooped to warm his hands. "The odd thing is," he said in a deliberately lightened tone, "I don't say I love you because, if I did, it certainly wouldn't be true—as you understand the word. And as for the word's other meaning, I'm not a fool. . . . But what is true," he went on, taking a match from a box and splitting it with his thumb-nail, "what is true," he repeated, and let the box fall and scatter, "is that I want more than anything on earth to be loved *by* you. *By* you," he said again. "We happen to have bodies, so there's that too. But if I hadn't a body or you hadn't, still— to be loved *by* you."

"But how can anyone want to be loved by a person whom they don't love?"

"That seems mad to you?"

"It seems—something outside experience."

"Remember," he said, "that any other man, feeling what I feel, would have said he did love you—any other man. He would probably have believed it; you, too, perhaps. I have told you what is really true."

"Why did you tell me?"

He smiled. "Words fix things. Once a thing is said, it comes out of the shadows. There it is—always. Five minutes ago, it didn't exist. Now it's a part of me and of you. Are you angry?"

"No." To avoid abrupt withdrawal, she let him take her hand.

"You're afraid still."

She rose and walked past him.

"You needn't be," he said. "I shall say no more of it."

She sank down on the window-seat, wishing the rain would stop. "Rain or no rain," she said, "I am going out before dinner."

"Do I come with you—or not?"

"Yes," she said; "will you?"

Others came with them. There was a rattling of sticks, a barking of dogs; outside was already a thickened dusk, soon they were walking in darkness, but they returned with faces whipped and a sense of having broken the imprisonment of the day. They were hungry; the cheerfulness and light raised the pitch of their voices; everyone, when they came down from their baths to the wood fire and the silver trays, seemed to be talking at once, and loudly, as if they were still talking against the howl of the wind. Severidge was telling them of Swedish iron-ore and of the journey he proposed to make to Stockholm. "I want Henry to come with me," he said. "Would that be allowed?"

24

WHEN Severidge proposed the journey to Henry by telephone, he accepted—then, as he was about to put down the receiver, asked to be given twenty-four hours to decide.

"Why?" Severidge asked impatiently. "What is there to prevent you? A moment ago you said 'yes'. What can have changed since then?"

The impatience of his tone put Henry on his mettle. "There's other work that may conflict," he said. "I can't be sure until to-morrow," and so, for the time being, it was left.

On his way home from the office that evening Henry tried to reach an understanding with himself. Hitherto he had swum vigorously with the Severidge tide. Why had he hesitated now?

When he reached Chelsea, he found Vivien by the fire, deep in a book, and, though it was dark outside, he said: "It's cold but there's no wind. There's more than an hour before we eat. Come for a walk."

They went beside the river under a weak, clouded moon, which gave pallor to the water but no gleam. Vivien was wearing a hooded coat and had drawn up the hood; only if she turned her head towards him was her face visible, but he took her arm, and, though they seldom saw each other and spoke little, they felt that they were nearer to each other than they had been for many days.

Henry's intention had been to tell her of the Stockholm proposal. It was in his mind that, if he refused it, she would be pleased, but this was no more than an intuition in him; it was opposed to the reason which told him that it was his duty to cultivate his alliance with C.M.I., and he was distrustful of his intuitions. Therefore, as they walked, he spoke of other matters when he spoke at all, and she waited in vain for him to say what was in his heart. At each struggle to speak he gathered her arm more closely to him, and at each failure to find words he lightened his hold again.

Since he had been threatened with disaster and had escaped, the knowledge that he owed his escape to chance and to no effort of his own had weighed heavily upon him. He had begun to understand how many of the criminal acts for which men were punished were not the result of a will to crime or even of criminal habit but were as astonishing to those who committed them as the discovery in one's own wardrobe of the clothes belonging to another man. He wanted Vivien to understand that the clothes were not his; he wanted her to feel that his inmost self was not affected by his guilt and was indeed the self she had loved. By nature very little introspective and by habit careful not to give an impression of sensitiveness, he was nevertheless far from being dull-minded—his air of gaiety and casualness being at once his self-protection and, towards the world, his contribution to good manners; and it was Vivien's recognition of the seriousness in him, which others missed and which he was content that they should miss, that had given their love, in his eyes, its distinguishing character. She was intellectually in advance of him; she was richer in talent, more articulate, and subtler in her response to human contacts. There were senses in which it might seem true to others that she was the leader, he the camp-follower, yet this had never been the nature of the relationship between them. Their love had its origin and strength in their being complementary in ways known to them only—in a secret equality, dwelling within their inequalities, which enabled them, whether they were serious or frivolous, whether they were passionately alone or laughing with or at each other in a general company, to preserve that mysterious sense of being at one, and of something unique and sacred in their unity, which children may have who love each other. This harmony, Henry knew, was threatened. By what? By the folly he had committed? And yet she had been unshaken by it. When he had first told her the truth, she had accepted it at once as though she herself had been a part of him, seeing through his eyes the world's sudden menace. Nor, since then, by any unkindness or coldness had she held aloof from him. Nevertheless, their former harmony was broken. The fault, he had argued, must be his, and he had tried to correct it by doing with all his might those things the neglect of which had brought disaster near, saying to himself that only unremitting work and professional success could restore their confidence. With all he did she had appeared to sympathize; she had encouraged and helped him, particularly in his work for Severidge. In spite of this they were not at one; they lived as if they were, and yet were not; it was as if they were gradually losing the language of their secret and so the power to revitalize it; their affection, their friendship, even their passion remained, but their marriage was dying.

If this had been true of a marriage, not their own, which they were observing, and he had been puzzled as he was now, he would have said to her: "Vivien, what do you suppose is wrong with that marriage?" and she, with her quickness of sympathy and understanding, would have given him an answer which, even if he did not at once agree with it, would have put his own judgment on the track; but now, try as he would, he could find no words, that did not seem disloyal or unloving, in which to express his disquiet. He could do no more than hold her arm, and feel for her hand, interlacing his gloved fingers with hers, and speak to her now and then on subjects very far from both their hearts.

At last, when they had almost reached Chelsea Bridge, he said:

"This evening at the office Severidge telephoned. He wants me to go to Stockholm with him."

"He said something of it at Felden," she answered.

"Of asking me to go with him? You didn't tell me."

"It was pretty vague," she said. "Are you going?"

"I haven't decided. I gather it wouldn't be for more than a week."

They walked on in silence. Henry was remembering the impatience of Severidge's voice on the telephone. If I indulge in moods, he said to himself, I shall lose the biggest client I have ever had, and, because he did not want to accept, it seemed to him that he ought not to refuse. Nevertheless, the recollection of Severidge's overbearing insistence and the discovery that it had needed courage to put down the receiver without yielding filled Henry with disquiet. Whether or not he went to Stockholm was a small matter, but the proposed journey was a link in a chain from which in his heart he wished to be free. And why, in heaven's name, if I wish to be free of it, do I do everything in my power to strengthen it? Apart from the ordinary work of solicitor for client, why do I give my time to working out a scheme for the Severidge Foundation, on which he has given me no formal instructions?

He drew Vivien aside to the Embankment wall.

"Listen to the river," he said.

They leaned against the parapet. Obviously, he thought, it's my job to go on with Severidge, whether I like it or not.

"Vivien," he said, "I wish you'd tell me something."

"Yes?" she answered. "I'll try."

"I suppose you have known all the time that I had one of my problems?"

"That was my idea," she admitted.

"All this time we've been walking in the dark, you have been waiting? I'm sorry. I have never been articulate."

"I have never minded that."

"Is there anything you do mind? Anything in particular, I mean?"

"Is that the problem?"

"I suppose it is. . . . Yes, it is. . . . In other words, am I doing—or not doing—anything that you——" He hesitated. "It's damned hard to say, Vivien, because I'm vague myself. I don't mean: am I doing anything that you don't like?—that's for me to find out. And I don't mean: am I doing anything of which you disapprove? I mean, I think, am I doing what you believe to be wrong? Is that a comprehensible question?" Before she could answer, he continued. "Once you said that I had what you called a 'deep-down'. It's a question of that, I suppose. . . . Oddly enough," he added, "it was in South Street you said that."

Even now he would not bring himself to speak of Severidge, nor could she answer with the truth that was in her. Seeing that Henry was in distress, she wanted only to give him reassurance. To censure him, to suggest that the work to which he was devoting himself and his whole association with Severidge were alien to their conception of their life together would, she felt, be cruel, and, in her, wilful and unreasonable.

"No," she answered, "you are doing everything on earth that you can do. Why should I feel it to be wrong?"

It was an answer that gave him no help—not the answer, he knew, that she would have given if they had been still in touch as once they had been—and yet, outwardly, it was satisfactory and final. Nothing was left for him to say except: "Then it's all right, I suppose."

Perhaps, he thought, it is all right. I'm over-sensitive or proud or something. It was perfectly normal that he should want me to go to Sweden with him. It's part of the whole job, and I had better go quietly on with it. Anyhow, it has, and can have, nothing on earth to do with Vivien and me. It's purely professional. Why am I making a mountain out of a mole-hill? What did I want her to say?

"Henry," she said lightly and in a quick voice as if to indicate that what she had to say now had no connexion with what had gone before, "I don't see why you should go to Stockholm. Do you want to?"

"Not in the least."

"Then why should you?"

"Only as part of the job."

"I see." She felt she had no right, because she had no reason, to dissuade him.

"Agreed?" he said.

"Yes," she answered. "It was only that it seemed to me——"

"What?"

"Rather a filthy journey in winter."

To this he made no reply. They came away from the parapet. As they turned to walk home, her face appeared to him from within her hood.

"I love you," she said in a tone of recognition, "with all my heart," but when he moved towards her, she took his arm instantly, laughed, and began to go forward.

Next morning, when he reached his office, he telephoned that it would be impossible for him to go to Stockholm. What link there was between this decision and his evening walk with Vivien he could not have said. The change of plan produced little effect. Afterwards they were no more at one than before; he did not even tell her that the decision was made until several days had passed. He had been careful to give a reason for his not going by which Severidge was satisfied. Except the staff that was to make this particular journey, nothing was changed.

25

THE Judge had thought it possible that he might stay in Greece until the New Year, but returned sooner. While Vivien had stood by Severidge's fire talking of Sweden, he was seated by a bedside table in an Athens lodging-house. He had closed a letter to his bank telling them to forward no more correspondence, and now wrote to his brother to announce his journey. This done, he put on a greatcoat which had been acting as coverlet to the bed, sat down again, wrapped a rug closely about legs and feet, and began to write. Presently he drew a table-lamp a few inches nearer to him, took off the shade, warmed his hands at the chimney, and dipped his pen again.

He had not intended to write *The Athenian* in Greece. His plan had been to make pilgrimages by coaster or across country —one, in particular, to Plataea, another to Delphi by the old road—and to use his eyes. He would try to see and smell and taste his period once more; his notes would be a diary of his Athenian's senses; he might even write a few passages, but they were to be no more final than the drawings made by a painter in the open air for a landscape to be carried out in his studio. This plan he had faithfully pursued while summer lasted, living much in the air, begging lifts when he needed them, sleeping under whatever cover he found, talking with all sorts and conditions of men. Though in Greece a talkative and friendly companion was never far to seek for a countryman of Lord Byron—Byron's name being a passport in that country which has the rare virtue of political gratitude—he was much solitary; and solitude, and later confinement by foul weather, had had their effect upon him: driven in upon himself, he had begun to write.

He wrote slowly and with extreme difficulty, but what he wrote ceased to be notes and became narrative. Ruefully at first, then with increasing independence, he became aware that no divine urgency drove his pen; by no means did his tale come to him, as poetry did to Keats, "as naturally as leaves to a tree"; the intellectual process remained conscious and deliberate. Nevertheless, there closed in about him as he wrote the walls of a room, tranquil and ageless, which excluded all consciousness except of his subject, and, as if the walls themselves were aglow, concentrated light upon it. The intellectual process, which these walls embraced, became intensified to the point of delight; his scholarship began to speak to him with an extraordinary intimacy, to reveal secrets to his intuition which, hours later, his reason tested, to confirm or to reject; and he had a sense of there having been made accessible to him a well upon which he might draw endlessly, though he must let down his bucket with as much care and draw it up with as much labour as ever, and be as cautious in his use of what it contained. So each day he went to the well eagerly; his pages multiplied until, turning over one afternoon what he had written the night before, he said to himself: I mustn't write more while I'm out of reach of my material. If I do, I shall begin to write thin. I must return to base while the going's good. He went at once to arrange his journey and the next evening wrote to Oxford and to his bank.

The little ship, *Melos*, the best he could afford, jogged home too slowly for him. His longing to be at work was like a desire for sleep; it knocked at his head; he saw his filing cabinets before him, rifled their treasures, and pursued with imagined precision the series of cross-references that would set at rest the problems now aching in his mind. When I get there, says the marching soldier to himself, I will sleep, I will sleep, I will sleep; no other word, no other image, appeases him; the idea of being ever again disturbed is blotted out. Gaskony's hunger was in the same kind. When I get there, he said, I will write.

The idea of postponement or interruption was intolerable. He saw himself in the room that Lou had promised. All his books and cabinets, overflowing to the box-room on the half-landing above, were waiting for him while the *Melos* rolled like an apple in the Bay, and he thought: when I get there, why should anyone be told that I am in England?

What a schoolboy plot—to lie doggo until it suited him to emerge! Impossible, he knew; letters had to be answered, Dick must be told, Vivien must be able to make touch; but the notion pleased him; so far as he could, he would give effect to it; and in London he unfolded it to Dick, who met him there. When he visited Vivien and Henry in Chelsea, he bound them to say nothing of his return.

"You mean," she said, "to Severidge?"

"To him least of all—but I mean to no one. I'm launched on my book. For a bit, I want to have it to myself."

"But if you are in London——"

"I shan't be."

"But you will need all your material. What about the Temple flat?"

This, he had known, would be difficult. He and Dick had conspired on the subject and his answer was ready: Dick had let the flat for him and moved his material out. This was blessedly true.

"Where?" said Vivien.

"For the time being at Lou's."

"At Cliftonville!"

"Better than a warehouse," he said. "More get-at-able. Besides, Lou has a classical spirit. She'll look after it."

"And you," Vivien asked, "where are you going?"

"Well," he said, "that's a bit awkward. You see, I'm back before my time. I shall go to Dick's for two nights. Then to Margate and see about things. Address me at Lou's; she'll forward if I move."

As he said these words, the whole conversation of which they were a part seemed to him false—as emptily plausible as one of the contrivances in a Restoration play. At the back of his mind had been a dread that when Vivien discovered his poverty, she would not accept it; she would blame herself and Henry; the whole episode of the wager would have to be dragged out of the past. Would it not have been simpler, nevertheless, to have told her the truth now and been done with it? Words formed in his brain—"the fact is, Vivien, I'm dead poor, and you may as well know it"—but he did not speak them, opportunity passed.

"Address me at Lou's" he repeated. "I'll keep in touch with her, and look you up whenever I pass through London."

Vivien was making fresh tea. The first brew had been watered and was no longer strong enough. Stooping beside the fireplace, she looked back over her shoulder, electric kettle in hand.

"In other words," she said, "you don't want to be bothered? Is that it? . . . But that's easy. That's an old pact between us."

How easy it was when she put it so! Even when she was a child, they had tacitly agreed to respect the independence of each other's lives. "Don't bother me!" had been a catchword of self-defence, mutually permitted. Blessed formula, rare in women!

Smiling back at her, Gaskony repeated it now, a saving incantation; but, as he repeated it and met her puzzled eyes, it became an echo from her childhood, and he remembered a disquieting phrase or two in her letters that had come to him in Greece.

"But you, my dear," he said, "are you all right? Tell me about yourself."

She hesitated for the time needed to pour milk into his cup. "Now, Gasky," she answered, "don't *bother* me! You go for a long walk with your Athenian and leave me to cast my own devils out."

26

CAMPION ROAD had not the commercial good fortune to stand upon the front at Cliftonville. When it was built on the grassy outskirts of the town in the direction of the North Foreland, it was able for a little while to advertise a "sea-view", but houses grander than its own sprang up among the mire and rubble which were then all that divided it from the esplanade, and Campion Road was shut in for ever. Its houses were of red brick and decorative stone. Its front yards, variously encouraged to bear grass or evergreens, were traversed by strips of tessellated pavement, in yellow, purple and terracotta, which enabled a visitor to walk daintily from gate to porch. Over each front door was a fanlight of coloured glass which bore in white letters the house's name. Number Eight was called Minerva. Its knocker was a brass owl.

"Lou," the Judge said when she admitted him, "you didn't have that knocker when I was here in the summer."

"There," she exclaimed, putting down the suitcase she had taken from his hand, "we were wondering how long it would be before you noticed that. It was William who found it. He saw it in a shop. 'Look, mother,' he said, 'there's an owl-knocker.' 'And what of it?' I said. 'Well, mother,' he said, 'an owl is Minerva's bird, and when Mr. Gasky comes—' So nothing else would do and there it is. You don't mind, Sir William, do you—the boy and I often call you 'Mr. Gasky' between ourselves. It was the nursery name, you see, and the boy has it from me."

A domed forehead and a pair of bare knees now appeared in the dark passage. Their owner was still for a moment but, when the Judge recognized him, came forward with a determined rush. With one hand he pushed away the hair that would have been on his forehead if his mother had not just plastered it back with a wetted brush; the other he held out; and he said—to be over and done with it: "Good evening, Sir William."

"Good evening, Will. Thank you for your knocker. It's a good welcome from Athens."

"Will you tell us about Athens?"

"I will, on condition that you and your mother call me by the old name—old to her, anyhow. You know, Lou, if you call me by the other, I shall have to go back and be a judge."

"Shall I take this?" asked William, lifting the suitcase.

"Yes," said his mother. "There's a good boy. You take Mr. Gasky to his room and I'll follow with a cup of tea. It's Minnie's afternoon, Mr. Gasky, that's how it is."

Boy and man went slowly up the flimsy staircase to a back room on the second floor. When Lou came up, she repeated an earlier offer to give Gaskony, during the winter, better accommodation at the same price—"then you could move in here," she said, "when we begin to fill up"; but Gaskony refused. "I want to get settled, Lou, with my books and things arranged as I want them. I want to feel I shan't ever have to move again."

When he was alone, he wondered whether, in fact, he would ever move again. Would he spend the rest of his life here? A sash-window looked out on to the back-yards of Campion Road and of the nameless road parallel to it. This window was in the centre of the wall. The space on its left held two of his filing cabinets; that on its right took the head of his bed. At the foot of the bed was a gas-fire, and beyond the fire a chest of drawers of grained varnish. Bed, fire and chest of drawers fully occupied the side-wall, and almost in the corner, but withdrawn a little so that the drawers could be opened without hitting it, was a washstand covered with white linoleum. All remaining wall-space, even that above the door, was occupied by bookshelves from the Temple, cut down under Dick's guidance to fit their new quarters and to include the filing cabinets as bricks include a door-frame. Only above the bed, the mantelpiece and the chest of drawers did wall-paper appear —a design of blue barges, trees, canals and windmills on a buff ground. Now where on earth, Gaskony thought, do I hang my overcoat? and he let it lie on the bed until a journey in quest of missing books revealed, in the box-room assigned to him, a wardrobe embedded among shelves. Having explored the box-room by candle-light, he returned to his own room. From the middle of its ceiling hung an old gas-bracket, now wired for electric light and fitted with two bulbs. The white blaze was little softened by shades of yellow silk and fell naked through the glass beads at their edges. Gaskony aimlessly switched off the light and switched it on again. If his table was to remain under the window—and it could stand nowhere else if it was to be a bed-table as well—he couldn't work with a central light. Besides, he hated a central light—the bane of bad hotels, the only stubborn barbarism of the French! I must have an oil-lamp, he thought. I can trim it myself if it makes work for Lou or Minnie. Then it struck him that Lou might not trust him with an oil-lamp; she was modern, she'd be afraid of fire; and in any case, he thought, if she hasn't got one I can't afford to buy a lamp. . . . That's odd.

He lay down upon his bed to try it: softer than his bed in Greece, but narrower than any he had slept on since he was a schoolboy in a dormitory. That was a long time ago. Holidays. Dick, Phil Brown, footsteps on the gravel, the surgery-bell. "Work hard, my boy, there are great prizes at the Bar. Some day you might be Lord Chief Justice." Sitting up on the bed, he noticed his tea-tray. He drank a cup cold, fearing that Lou might be hurt by neglect of her kindness, and began then to unpack and put away his clothes. In the chest of drawers he found a picture lying on its face. It was his little Sickert pastel of a girl in a white dress, Vivien's gift, and attached to it was a label on which was written: "I thought you would like to hang this for yourself. The wall-paper's pretty grim." So Dick had saved that from the wreck! Gaskony balanced it on the mantel-piece and gazed until he dared to gaze no longer. He turned abruptly to face the room—the high blaze of electricity, the sharp, still shadows, the thin rug, the stained boards. For the first time with full recognition he saw this room not as a place he was visiting but as his home. He began to shiver. Fool, it's December and there's no fire. He knelt on the rug, struck a match and turned on the tap, but the fire did not light, and he wondered whether he was being stupid about the mechanism of the thing. Was there another tap? Sitting back on his heels, he looked for it in vain. Then he saw the meter, put on his spectacles, read the instructions. There was a shilling in his pocket and he plunged it experimentally into the slot. When he had obeyed Instructions B and C, the fire, to his satisfaction and surprise, burned.

Supper came on a tray: fish, boiled potatoes, cabbage, a tinned pear. Afterwards he went downstairs to talk to Lou in the kitchen, carrying his tray. William was engaged in a Latin prose and they discussed the ways of avoiding *ut* with the subjunctive. Lou knitted and told him how Vivien, without his knowing it, had fallen from a house she had built in a tree; she told him also where the post-office was and where to find a shop in which he might buy ink—"really, Mr. Gasky," she reproved him, "one might think you had come to Darkest Africa!" But she forgivingly promised him a waste-paper basket and described her only other lodgers at present: a delicate little girl—"come for the air"—and her grown-up sister, "a very nice young lady". They played ping-pong of evenings, but, as they had the first-floor front, Mr. Gasky wouldn't be disturbed by them.

He enjoyed sitting with Lou by the kitchen range, and, as he told her his working routine, his spirits rose. She had an oil-lamp; she would trim it now, and he should take it upstairs when he went to bed. That there was a lamp after all gave him keen pleasure; it seemed to him an omen; as though it had been awaiting his need, it annulled his sense of being outcast. While he watched the hands filling and wiping it, as though they were impersonal hands less real than the lamp itself, he looked up at Lou's straight dark brows and the little mole on her left cheek and thought gladly: While I am climbing the stairs, it is her life that will be continuing here; here, in Lou, will be the centre of all time and space, as it was in my Athenian, and in Nausicaa when Odysseus climbed on to her beach. He took the lamp, said good-night, and started on his way. Now if only I could get that on to paper, he thought, then my book wouldn't be a period piece; it would be timeless-true from the inside outwards. Upstairs, in his striped pyjamas, he said his prayers for custom's sake. He said them standing, as he was about to get into bed: first, "Lighten our darkness . . .", fast and silently, then his own aloud—six monosyllables used every night for over fifty years: "God, make me fit to write." Before he was fourteen, he had asked: "O God, help me to write a great book," but, in his fifteenth year, had amended the plea. "God, make me fit to write," he said now, and slid between sheets. God, who could read shorthand, would not object to this: it was not a demand-note; it was not a prayer for results. It was from the inside outward, as near as he could make it; and left to the Court a wide and, he hoped, a merciful discretion.

27

DECEMBER and January passed but Vivien came no nearer to casting out her devils. She and Henry did not take the holiday they had promised themselves at Christmas-time; when she reminded him of it, he said that it wouldn't be easy to leave London, and by common consent they let the subject drop. They were entertained often by Severidge and by the men of power to whom he introduced them. From the centre of the circle thus formed she watched Henry at the circumference of it and began to feel that she was watching him no longer with her own eyes but from under the dropped lids, from within the alien pouches. Even her own body was separated from her. When Severidge, helping her into a cloak, let the back of his hand rest, and move, upon her bare shoulder, and when, a moment later, he searched in her eyes for recognition of the caress, her body said to her: Who are you? and that night, when she and Henry were in their flat, she pulled out a book, opened it, shut it again and said:

"Why didn't Severidge fight in the last war?"

"I don't know. Why?"

"I thought everybody volunteered." She rose from the chair-arm. "I'm going to have a bath."

"At two in the morning?"

"I am going to have a bath," she insisted, emphatically separating the words. "Put on a dressing-gown and come and talk to me."

He carried in an ash-tray and sat beside the bath, smoking a cigarette.

"Do you suppose," she asked, "that Gasky's going to *live* in that place of Lou's?"

"Have you heard from him again?"

"Only once since he came up after Christmas. He says he's working. But he can't *live* in Margate, surely?"

"Do you miss him, Vivien? Is that the trouble?"

She lifted her face out of the sponge. "Miss him? No. We have never clung."

"Do you want to go down and see him?"

"When he wants me."

"I thought," said Henry, "that might be—partly—why you are on edge."

She turned on to her face and was silent while she rippled the water over her shoulders. "You know," she said, "we're not his kind of people."

"Whose kind? Gasky's?"

"Oh God," she said, "we're his kind all right! I'd come out of Margate long ago."

Henry's smile was that with which he always confessed himself a laggard when she went too fast for him.

"I mean," she said, "in the next war you will fight. . . . Give me my towel." While he was reaching for it, she was out; her wet cheek touched him. "If, when it comes, anyone says: 'Don't fight'—" She started again. "If, when it happens, I say: 'Don't'—beat me or drown me."

"Sounds improbable," he answered.

"I wonder. I'm changing, you know. So are you. Doesn't it frighten you? . . . Henry, what are we doing on the eighth?"

He was bewildered, counting the days. "That's nearly a fortnight ahead."

"Get your engagement-book—please!"

He went and returned with it. "Nothing special. There's a C.M.I. subcommittee at three. I'm invited as a kind of observer, and——"

"Have you forgotten Glasgow?"

Gazing, he remembered. "But, Vivien, it's impossible to go out of London then. On the ninth——"

"Not impossible," she said. "Necessary."

"Of course," he admitted, "we must call on the old lady, but that particular day——"

"You promised."

"But why the eighth?"

"She chose it. I don't know why. The Queen of Scots was executed on that day."

"Was she? How did you find that out? Even so——"

"You promised." She wrapped her dressing-gown over her. "Promise me. You wouldn't come away at Christmas-time. Now——"

"But why?"

"Promise! Not to go would be—promise, promise—it's what we were—it's a *thing!* Henry!"

This he took seriously. "All right," he said. "Night train on the seventh. You had better send a note to remind her."

" 'You are too English'!" she exclaimed. "The great lady doesn't need to be told."

But he went to Glasgow reluctantly, thinking of the engagements he had cancelled, courteously not speaking of them. This journey was to have been for her—if such things were still possible—one of their queer, personal festivals. Recognizing this, he had tried to live up to it, and had bought her a book, for inscriptions in books celebrated their festivals, and had written in it Mary Stuart's motto: " 'My end is in my beginning,' February 8, 1587–1935." She smiled and kissed him for it, but the journey disappointed them. Mrs. Gorsand was indeed expecting their arrival; she was welcoming and shrewd; but Vivien had come too much as one looking for a sign, and received none.

When the visit was over and their train drew out of Glasgow, she said:

"Sorry, Henry, I have wasted your time. It wasn't a *thing* after all. I oughtn't to have been there."

"Why not you?"

"Not in my present mood. She had nothing to say to us. If she had, we couldn't take it. She was disappointed too."

Henry moved uneasily. She knew that he was looking for an answer that would make her feel that she had not failed, but he was helpless and began to open his newspaper. For more than an hour they were silent.

"She didn't speak of Severidge," he said, leaning forward.

"No." He leaned back into his corner again, but she touched his knee to recall him. "As a matter of fact, she did ask me whether he kept his Cennini in a glass case."

"Does he?"

"At Felden."

"I haven't seen it."

"The case has been finished since you were last there."

Henry made a reply that she could not hear against the drumming of the wheels. She asked what he had said, but he moved his hand to and fro between them in sign that it was not worth repeating.

In London, he had a dinner engagement for which it was not necessary that he should dress. They separated at the station. At the flat she made herself tea but ate nothing. She looked up in the telephone-book the number of the club at which, she knew, Henry was dining, but, as soon as the ringing began, hung up the receiver. Among the heap of waiting letters, she sorted Henry's from her own. Severidge's handwriting made her tremble, but she saw at once that his letter was short; an invitation, presumably, and not about the loneliness of power or the—but it was odd, what he had to say:

I think you ought to go to Cliftonville. Did you know he was there? I suppose you did. For all I knew he was still in Greece, until I found out by chance. He has resigned from Rodd's—that gave me the hint—and I have had inquiries made. He isn't ill, at least I don't think so, but something odd has happened. It is very disquieting. I was fond of him —you know that, though once I believe you thought otherwise—and I shall go to Cliftonville to-morrow, the eleventh, but I don't want to butt in alone. Will you come?

Or would you rather I stood aside while you went alone?
As you decide. But someone ought to go. Ring me when
you get this.

She telephoned and listened to what he had to say. His information was—"what information?" she asked. He laughed:
"Didn't you know I had a tame intelligence service?" . . . His
information was, he continued, that Gasky lived in a single
room at the back of a cheap lodging-house. Shabby—carefully
brushed, but shabby. Bought nothing, no drink, no tobacco,
nothing. Went to the Public Library on Fridays to have a look
at *The Times*. Gave Latin lessons to little boys. Locally, called
the Old Miser. . . . "No tobacco!" Severidge exclaimed. "No
newspaper of his own. No companions. No talk—it doesn't
sound like the Judge. Resigned from Rodd's. What d'you make
of it?"

Without waiting for her answer, he gave his operation orders.
He would drive her down in his car to-morrow. He must
return to London the same night, but she had better bring a
suitcase; she might wish to stay.

"But what has happened? You say he's not ill."

"No, but he's a kind of prisoner as far as I can make out—
or thinks he is."

"What nonsense! What kind of a prisoner can he be?"

"To be frank, I think he's a bit touched."

Vivien asked impatiently: "Why?"

"The way he's living is flat contrary to everything that——"

"But he's not poor," Vivien said.

"My dear, I know that. I know that. But he's living like
death. That is what makes me think— Well, come and see for
yourself."

At breakfast she told Henry that she was going to see Gasky
and might stay a night. Well, Henry thought, it's no earthly
good trying to prevent her. Gasky's had his run. I'd have told
her at the beginning if I'd had my way.

28

WITH a little difficulty Vivien persuaded Severidge not to take her to the most gilded of the hotels but to another of more moderate splendour which nevertheless overlooked the sea. She would have liked to know what form his inquiries had taken—had he dispatched secretaries to track Gasky? what means of information had he?—but he turned her tentative questions by making her feel that she was guileless in asking them. He would not tell her that he had obtained the forwarding address in Campion Road from the Judge's bank, which was his own and to him not secretive; therefore, he would tell her nothing of methods, only of results; and this she had learned to accept from him. He traded in results, he waved wands.

At heart, she knew that he waved them destructively over her marriage, and not the less because, by his patronage of Henry, he fostered its prosperity; but she was learning to ridicule her own sense of danger as men learn always to ridicule the values they are forsaking. Prompted by Severidge's reverence for her "goodness"—as though it were the beauty of another age to be kept in a glass case and secretly fondled— she had begun, in defiance, to regard critically the happiness which she had known, and accused herself of having been ingenuously sentimental. This self-accusation, as much as her genuine wish not to "bother" Gasky, had kept her away from Margate hitherto, and had presented to her, in the mocking guise of "keepsake", not only the book that Henry had bought for her Glasgow journey, but, in swift humorous retrospect, other books, remembrances, tokens, sacred follies which had marked their private festivals. Comedy yields its truth only to those who are deep-founded in their own; others it flatters to applaud their lies. It has two spirits: the corrosive and the healing, Wycherley's and Goldsmith's, and Severidge had yawned at *She Stoops to Conquer;* in *As You Like It,* he had admired only the performance of Rosalind, shrugging at the play. Her taste for these pieces was, he had said, a part of her "goodness". Let her come to *The Country Wife* with him! They had gone in company; at supper, Henry, taunted for his disliking, had said: "Manure and cream!" and she had heard her laugh in the laugh that went against him. "But, Vivien, did you like it yourself?" Myself? Myself? My*self*? Who am I? She had been angry with him because he pressed her.

At luncheon, in the hotel's dining-room, she remembered that supper-party, and her face clouded. Severidge interpreted her mood as one of anxiety for the Judge and applied himself to reassure and divert her. "I expect," he said, "that the information I had exaggerates the whole thing. In any case, if, when we get there, anything is wrong, you are not to worry about it. Everything that can be done, shall be. Put your mind at rest." His words took effect; she was rocked by them as a child is rocked in its cradle; her mind was put at rest, not only on Gasky's account, but on her own; the supper-party was forgotten. "You know," Severidge was saying, "that husband of yours has a very remarkable capacity—anyhow, as far as I am concerned. Months ago, I spoke to him vaguely of a scheme I had in mind—the Severidge Foundation. . . . But perhaps he spoke to you of it?"

"Yes," she answered. "He was working on it."

"He was indeed! I gave him no instructions. What he did, he did on his own initiative. The other day he brought me a complete scheme worked out in detail. What did I think of it? I confess that at first I thought he was taking rather much on himself. It was a pet idea of mine, very personal to me, and, apart from that one talk, I hadn't been consulted. . . . However, I began to read his scheme. It was fascinating; it was like reading something I had drafted myself—a development, stage by stage, of my own thought—but making clear and concrete what had been for me not much more than a dream-in-outline. Now a man like that is what men like me search for in vain. Not a stenographer, not an agent who is always running back for orders, and not one of those thrusting blunt-heads who *do* things but do them not in my way. Henry does the thing and gives me the feeling of having done it myself. It's as if I had been inside his mind while he worked."

"I'm glad you're pleased," Vivien answered. "Poor Henry set great store by that scheme. He was always working at it—whenever other things gave him time to breathe."

"Why do you say 'Poor Henry'?"

"Did I say that? I don't know why."

"He is by no means 'poor Henry'," Severidge told her. "He has a great future if he cares to follow it. But he must see where his future lies. He must give himself room to grow. All that family-lawyer business that he clings to with half his mind will have to be let go. That's up to you, Vivien."

"Does he know you approve this scheme?"

"Not yet. I wanted to talk to you first. I have every intention of going forward on the lines he has laid down. It's a scheme on a very big scale; it will need Cabinet approval and an Act of Parliament—an agreed Act. Henry," he added with a glint of ironic admiration as though he were praising a schoolboy's epic, "Henry has even drafted the Bill. . . . Well, when the thing goes through, I want him to run it, and, seeing that it touches the Dominions and links up with the United States and Europe, that will mean his going abroad a good deal."

He searched her face.

"What about Bright, Lerrick?" she said. "He has a new partner, but in effect Bright, Lerrick's a one-man show."

"That's the point," Severidge answered. "Bright, Lerrick shrinks a bit."

"But it's his job."

"Oh no, it isn't. That's what you have to make him see. The other's bigger."

"Bigger," she repeated. Then, as if she were pleading a cause already lost: "But Bright, Lerrick is his!"

"So was his baby's rattle—once."

For Severidge the matter was settled. He paid the bill, and slid the change at the waiter. They made ready and walked out of the hotel. At sight of his car, she said: "Can we walk? It's not far to Campion Road."

He looked at his watch. "By all means. There's a stiffish breeze."

A wind off the land was turning back the wave-crests. They walked leaning against it, and Severidge, in his manner of guiding and guardianship, took Vivien's arm and closed his fingers about it a few inches above the wrist, impelling her. This physical contact, the pressure of his arm against her side, her sense of being conveyed, began to fret her body, then her mind. Severidge was talking to her eagerly, between the wind-gusts, of the part that she also must take in the Foundation that Henry had planned. Industry, he said, was not only ill-organized internally, but was out of touch with the non-industrial aspects of the community's life. This he proposed to remedy, and he spoke of how, in the modern world, the liberal arts must be cultivated collectively, how the fatal individualism of artists must be harnessed to citizenship, and how industry must contribute to this reorientation of ideas by taking a long, unselfish view of its responsibility. The Foundation, he said, was not to be regarded as a charitable one, nor as providing a substitute for private patronage of the arts. It was, rather, an acceptance of industry's obligations under a system of private enterprise, and its approach to the liberal arts was international as a socialistic approach to them could not be while governments were primarily nationalistic. Industry and banking had advanced much further than government on the path of inter-nationalism, and it was, therefore, natural and appropriate that industry should guide and guard the international development of the liberal arts. To guide this development was, in the long run, to guide the development of men's minds and—

To guide the development of men's minds, Vivien's thought

[147]

repeated. She listened no more to his words, though from time to time she answered a question or encouraged him to continue. The vast ambition of his plan stretched out before her like a desert in an insane dream. To guide the development of men's minds, to collectivize art and scholarship, to harness them to industry. . . . Across the desert a wind was blowing; the dust rose into her face, a paper bag swirled between her feet, she put down her head and struggled. The fingers on her arm tightened their grip, the thrust behind her elbow increased. . . . Henry had planned this desert; Henry had made it in another's image. "It's as if I had been inside his mind while he worked," Severidge had said.

"Of course," Severidge was saying now, "the fruit won't be gathered in my lifetime or in yours. But it is not impossible by planting the seed now to make pretty sure what crop international civilization will yield in the future—whether, to put it crudely, the liberal arts are to become more and more a decoration and die away into mere dilettantism or whether they are to be not only mass-distributed by radio and television but mass-produced—by which I mean produced not by the few for the few but by mankind for mankind."

Vivien was listening again now. He spoke of this commanded future as though it were a property of which he possessed a map; not with the wild, vague enthusiasm of a dreamer but as if an option on the property had already been bought, and he, a chairman in possession of the facts, were reporting on them to a docile assembly of shareholders. How docile they were—and she! For a moment her step faltered and the muscles of her arm tautened, but she did not after all disengage her arm from his. Was the fault hers? Perhaps he was justified in saying that, in a collectivized world, art must cease to be individualistic and self-regarding, and must "approximate more and more closely to the condition of industry". Was it true? Did circumstances make true what she herself felt to be a lie? Millions throughout the world could be persuaded into thinking so; it would not be hard for Severidge "to guide the development of men's minds" and to make them feel at once safe and enterprising as they struggled on, head down, into the desert wind.

"It must be about here," Severidge said, "that we turn in from the front if we are to strike Campion Road."

They were going to see Gasky, Vivien remembered. Her disengaged hand came up, felt under her coat, and encountered the hardness of the little diamond clip which had been given her, at the Red House, on the last anniversary of her mother's birthday. The conversation she and Gasky had then had about Severidge flooded back to her. The arm now pressing against her side was Severidge's. Why was she in Margate with him? Why was she going to visit Gasky in his company? With whose mind was she thinking? With whose feet was she walking? Where am I? Who am I? What have I become?

And yet she was English enough to suffer and deny much, rather than exhibit her moods. As she was, in fact, walking along the front at Cliftonville with Severidge, she had better continue to do so. What possible excuse had she for changing her plan now? Was she to make some hysterical and unaccountable scene? Certainly not. Having come so far, she would go on.

She went on. "Yes," she said. "I should think we must be about level with Campion Road."

"I have the map quite clear before me," he answered. "We shan't be wrong. Turn in here."

He drew her arm towards him as if it were a tiller. At the edge of the asphalt was a shelter of wood and glass, open four ways. In two of its armed seats, facing the sea and so protected from the wind, were a nursemaid deep in a magazine and a pale-faced, yellow-haired little girl, idle, bored, dangling her feet.

Vivien stopped and let Severidge's arm fall. Quite easy. No need to make a scene. Why had she thought a scene necessary? There was no need to tell him that she didn't want to walk across the desert, or to visit Gasky in his company, or to be thrust by his mind or his arm.

"I think I won't come now," she said. "I am tired. You go on alone."

He was full of solicitude. He would wait with her. He would go back and bring the car.

"No," she said, "please not. I'm perfectly all right. Just tired suddenly. I can go to see Gasky later to-day. To-morrow perhaps. If anything is wrong, it may be better you should find out first what it is."

She sat down in the shelter, two places dividing her from the little girl. Severidge stood before her.

"What *is* the matter?" he said.

"Nothing."

"Really nothing?"

"Nothing at all."

"Then change your mind and come. It's not five hundred yards." He held out his hand.

Her wrists were curved over the arms of her seat and exerted pressure on the wood as if she were about to rise, but she held herself back.

"No," she said. Then, quickly: "Better not tell Gasky I'm here. He'd think it odd, my not coming."

"I think so too," he answered, half holding out his hand. It was the first time that she had seen him irresolute.

She shook her head and smiled, and soon he was gone. She was looking uninterruptedly at the white lines of the wave-crests thrown back, and loosened all the muscles of her body. The little girl said: "Oh, what a big sigh!"

"Now, Millicent," said the nursemaid, "don't you go interfering."

29

THERE were times when Severidge needed company as other men need drugs. The desire for it swept upon him in waves, beating him down until he saw the whole world from within an agony of loneliness. This desire came upon him now. Between the shelter in which he had left Vivien and a row of boarding-houses looking out upon the sea lay a wide, open space of tufted grass. This was crossed by an asphalt path beside which, at equal intervals, were wire baskets for refuse. To walk up this path alone required of him the sternest compulsion of his will. He dared not look back at the shelter. If he had, he would have returned to it. Even to think of the possibility of returning was to feel again the pressure of Vivien's body against him and, in imagination, to bury his face in her and obliterate his loneliness in the smell of the coat she was wearing.

He went on up the path. Even the tufted grass, like the wooden shelter and the sea and the man who was posting a letter in a pillar-box far away, seemed to belong to an order of existence which excluded him. When he turned aside to rub down the grass with his foot, it sprang up again: to-night, when he was gone, it would wave on in the ground wind, and the careless sea would suck at the beach. A woman with a perambulator on her way towards the sea passed so close to him that the corner of his outblown overcoat touched the perambulator's springs, but, though he looked into the woman's face, she did not notice him. It was as if he were invisible, and life were going on in his absence. He wished to be seen, spoken to and touched, to establish communication between himself and the responseless world. He stopped by a refuse basket and dropped into it an envelope that was screwed up in the fingers of his right hand. The ball of paper blew into the corner of the basket and lay still.

Beyond the refuse basket some boys were playing "touch". He left the path, walked towards them, stood and watched. If Vivien had been there he would have said: I used to play that game as a boy, but as she was not there he was sucked into his boyhood and began to play the game in his mind. His game varied in detail from that which the boys were now playing but was of the same kind. He, being fast and agile, was "He"; the others were against him—they the pursued, he the pursuer. Their object was to get from their "base" between two ash-trees to their "home", an oak; his to touch, and so capture, as many as he could, while they were on their way. There were intermediate stages at each of which they might rest, invulnerable, until another claimed it, or until, by challenge from an allowed distance, the pursuer drove them out; but two might not share a refuge—as a second came, the first must take his risk in the open. Then "He" would pounce and capture him. By these captures, the number of the pursued was reduced, and the game would be repeated until but one remained to fight his way home if he could. Then "He" would face the surviving quarry in a final duel, giving him what space the rules required, manœuvering him from refuge to refuge, tempting him by withdrawal, or by pursuit edging him away from the oak-tree or forcing him out of bounds.

Standing on the tufted grass, Severidge forgot the boys he saw but heard their shouting. Their cries of escape and surrender, borne upon the wind, came to him out of his childhood and with them the rapture of his agility, his knowledge that he was swifter and more intelligent than any, his love of the rôle of pursuer which others gregariously shunned. When the game was over, he would mix with them and buy them ices on their way back, but he was not of them; he was on the fringe of their groups, and soon, when he seemed fastened to it, each group would dissolve and the boys of which it had consisted would drift away, in pairs or singly, some because they were made uneasy by the stab of his intelligence, some because they were indeed boys, drifting, malleable children, and did not feel that he, with his hard edges, was of the same species with themselves. They went their own ways from him as though he had been a greyhound walking in their company.

Now the boys he was watching ended their game. Light was failing. The wind hardened, and dusk began to seep through, rather than overspread, the wintry afternoon. They buttoned their jackets and set out homeward across the grey bents. As they passed near him, he said in a friendly way that the game had been played differently in his day; if they had responded he would have bought sweets for them on their way back. Heads turned, eyes looked at his boots, his overcoat, but did not meet his eyes. Perhaps the wind had carried his words away. He smiled and was about to speak again when the group broke up, farewells were shouted, and the boys drifted away, singly or in pairs, and began to run.

He turned sharply, regained the asphalt, walked on. Can you tell me, please, the way to Campion Road?

Rain was falling, the tessellated pavement was slippery. He rang. There was a long silence. He knocked with the owl. Boots slid towards him on linoleum. The boy who opened the door stared and wasn't sure. "Say Mr. George Severidge."

He waited by the hat-stand. What a place to go mad in! The clean squalor of it, the smell of soap and fish! What was the Judge doing here? What am I doing here? But when the boy leaned over the banisters and said: "Yes, please sir, will you come up?" Severidge, climbing the narrow stairs, felt in his spine and at the back of his knees the tremor of the hunt, as though the quarry were twisting under his hand, and, as he entered the room and saw its congested poverty and the Judge in its midst, he was seized by such a conflict of desire—to be this man's master and to be recognized and liked by him—that he forgot the words of encounter which he had prepared and said only:

"Who was that boy?"

[153]

"My landlady's son—William Vivien. We do Latin together."

"Your name and hers?" Severidge blurted out. "William and Vivien. Is that a coincidence?"

"No. She was Vivien's nurse. . . . But sit down. That is the best chair I can offer you. I was having tea. I don't provide for tea-parties but there's a spare cup. I keep it for William on occasions."

The cup was brought down from the chest of drawers. A tray stood on the floor between their chairs. The room was murky; day hung there still, but like a cobweb, through which a lamp on the window-table cast an indecisive light. Tea was poured out. Severidge felt that it was necessary for him to explain his visit, but he was embarrassed by his sense of having intruded upon the Judge's shame.

"I wouldn't have come," he said, "anyhow, not unannounced, if I had known——"

"You mean it's a small box? I felt that at first. Don't feel it now. It's difficult to have the window open without a draught on your head. Apart from that, it has its advantages—everything within reach."

Gaskony was polite, even cordial, but so impersonal that Severidge began to wonder whether he had grasped who his visitor was or did not, at any rate, periodically forget that this was he, Severidge, in the room. When he mentioned Rodd's and certain members by name, the Judge replied intelligently but without curiosity; the subject died, and Severidge thought: his mind is wandering; but there were moments in which he thought otherwise and felt that the Judge's detachment was a pretence to safeguard his poverty, or his miserliness, from humiliation.

At last he said: "What has happened, Judge?"

"Happened? In what way?"

"Resigned from Rodd's, living like this, I mean——"

"That is very simple. I have no money."

"But you have your pension."

"No."

Severidge was frightened by this monosyllable and by the

way in which it was spoken. There was neither protest nor regret nor resignation in the word; it was spoken historically, as if the speaker were unaffected by it; and Severidge, at the back of whose mind the idea that the Judge was wrong in his head still powerfully lingered, was appalled to find that it was possible for a man, while appearing sane, to acknowledge abject poverty as though that poverty were not his. He wished to drag the Judge back from his delusion, as he would have wished to drag back on to dry land some wretch who was drowning before his eyes and who would be for ever the grateful creature of his deliverer; and he said, therefore:

"But that can't be true. Government pensions don't cease." And he added in the soothing tone of a sick-nurse: "Try to tell me how it happened."

Gaskony was silent a moment. "Yes," he said with a smile. "I will tell you. It will interest you. My pension went as part of the price of *Marius the Epicurean*. . . . But tell me, why have you come?"

The name of the book and the sudden question struck at Severidge like two dagger-thrusts. He did not know why he had come—whether it was to peer at the downfall of a man he hated and regather him into his power, or to gain admittance to an individuality he envied and would be loved by. The words he wished to speak—wished passionately to speak as though they were tears to be shed—were: "I have your *Marius!*" but he answered sedately:

"I came, my dear Gaskony, to ask how you were."

"You see how I am," the Judge returned. "When the time came to return the purchase price of *Marius*, the money had been spent. It had to be found. So you see how I am."

"She doesn't know this?"

"Who?"

"Vivien."

The Judge jerked his head at the name. "In fact, she doesn't. Why do you ask?"

"She mustn't know."

"On the contrary. I have kept her ignorant too long. I wanted to be sure of myself first. Weakness in me," Gaskony said. "You tell her when you get back to London. Tell her what the place looks like. Tell her to come and see for herself. She and I have a rule—not to bother each other."

"A discreet rule I should imagine between guardian and ward."

"Not only," said Gaskony. "I mean," he added, "it is a saving rule between man and man—I think, between soul and soul. If only the immortal gods had observed it, there'd have been less muddle on Olympus! I believe that, in fact, the gods do observe it—pretty well; though man, the busybody, imagines them otherwise."

With such a match as this the Judge had been accustomed to light the conversational fuse at Rodd's, and for a moment Severidge was reassured, but silence followed; he felt again that he was forgotten and that the Judge had eluded him, sliding back into a world of his own. He took out his cigarette-case and offered it.

Gaskony shook his head. "Cured of that."

"Why?"

"Each of them costs two newspapers. Not that I take a newspaper."

"But why not? It's ridiculous."

"Well," said Gaskony, "they cost money. The Athenians, a highly political people, did without them. What paper I buy, I write on."

"But books?" Severidge exclaimed.

Gaskony's hand moved through the air. "There is also a box-room; and a public library."

Severidge stood up. "Do you know," he began, "I don't mind confessing to you: when I came here, I thought you were—well, not mad but touched."

"That doesn't astonish me."

"But you're sane enough to pull my plutocratic leg."

"But what I have said is true."

"I know. I know it's true. I don't mean that you were pulling my leg in that sense—only that your rattling of an empty pocket was a bit of millionaire-baiting. You wouldn't have rattled it at anyone else."

Gaskony grinned. "You know a lot."

"Vivien said that to me once."

Gaskony nodded calmly. "It's a family catchword. What did you answer?"

"I said: 'Yes, but not enough.'"

"That answer," Gaskony replied, "will go to your credit in heaven."

"Not much good to me," said Severidge, "if I don't get there to draw on the account."

The window was by now altogether dark and Gaskony drew the curtains over it. His visitor, watching him closely, took in the finality of what he saw—the pinched writing-table, the threadbare curtains, the narrow cottage bed with its coverlet of some glossy material not silk; they were not Gaskony's prison only, for there was no release from them; they were his grave. This was the condition to which his pride was reduced; this was what his integrity had come to! He who had made a virtue of refusing to sell his *Marius* at any price, and then had sold it to satisfy some debt hanging round that upright neck, was now condemned to this lodging-house. Severidge was uneasily triumphant in the spectacle, as men, perhaps, have been triumphant in the sight of their enemy on the scaffold; and, observing it, bracing himself to be satisfied, he felt, as they may have done, that the victim was passing beyond reach. This misgiving represented itself to him, as it has represented itself to many a mob round many a scaffold, as the emotion of pity; he wanted to exercise the arrogance of pardon, to drag the victim back, to have him in his grip again— even to be reconciled with him and enjoy the submission of his gratitude, and the friction of these desires touched him with what seemed to be a generous warmth. How splendid to be the messenger spurring in with a reprieve! How glorious to wave the wand that produced a happy ending! How pleasant to know that Gaskony would be bound ever afterwards to acknowledge his goodwill and admit him to the equality of friendship!

"Listen, Gaskony," he said, "I have a proposition to make."

The Judge came back a step from the window and sat down on the edge of the bed.

"I know inside me," Severidge continued, "what your answer will be—your first answer, your first impulse, and I beg you not to make it. Can you open your mind—let the thing come quite fresh? Put away pride and convention. Then answer. . . . I want you to let me put an end to all this. Let me pay back the money."

"You don't owe it to me," the Judge said.

"I only put it that way," Severidge explained, with embarrassment, "in order to avoid saying—what I thought might make it, for you, harder, but I'll say it plainly: I want you to accept from me twenty-five thousand pounds." Without giving time for answer his words rushed on: "Come out of this now. Put what is necessary into a bag. By the time that is done, I'll have my car at the door." Severidge left the fireplace, skirted their two chairs, and stood beside the bed. "Decisions worth making are made at once. You say: yes. You leave this place. Your books and papers shall follow you. To-night we dine at Rodd's. Let me do that."

The Judge shook his head.

"Let me do that!" Severidge repeated, his fingers closing and unclosing on his shirt-cuffs. "The sum is nothing to me. This place is intolerable. You can't live here day after day until you die, sleeping in that bed, wasting your life."

"But I am happy here," Gaskony answered.

"You say so. You are bound to say it because you won't take money from me. . . . Judge, listen. We are very much alone in this room. Can't we for once, quite simply, stand clear of the gentlemanly rules? Don't, on a point of honour, deny the misery of this place. Why, in God's name, should you, who see deeper into life than most men, attach this wild, mad importance to money? A woman must starve rather than accept money: you must lie and go on living like a dog in a kennel rather than accept money: money is linked up in the conventional mind with fantastic notions of chivalry and honour. But it isn't important in that way. There's neither virtue nor vice in it. If someone died—if I died—and left you twentyfive thousand to-morrow, do you think you'd stay here? If by picking up a stone on the beach you could rescue yourself from this, you'd stoop down and pick it up. Money's no more—morally it's no more than that stone, intrinsically it's neither good nor evil. And yet, when I kick the stone your way, you turn up your nose and say: 'I'm happy here'. It's not stoicism, it's madness. Can't you see that? . . . Of course you see it. I beg you—have the courage to acknowledge it."

"But you are wrong," Gaskony answered. "You are wrong. I should not pick up the stone. I should come back here, live as I am living"—he touched the writing-table—"and go on with my book."

To Severidge this was no more than the same perverse pride that had compelled Gaskony for so long to stand out against a sale of *Marius*. He read it as a stubborn exclusiveness, a falsely patrician contempt for him and his money as untouchable, and it angered him; it vexed his self-esteem, it exasperated his reason, and his knuckles whitened. When he made his offer, he had desired to beat down Gaskony's pride for reasons of power that represented themselves to him as reasons of pity; he had made the offer glowingly and was stung now by what seemed to him ingratitude. Partly for this reason and partly because he was never able to deceive himself for long, the glow of pity faded. Only to fools is their self-deception opaque; the intelligent are soon tormented by its translucency; and to Severidge the motive of power became visible through the veil of compassion. For an instant he saw himself intolerably as one who was indeed outcast and predatory; and the anger against Gaskony, which a moment sooner had whitened his knuckles, swelled in him, and became a wrath against man that rejected him, a rage against the gods who had designed and set their mark upon him. This wrath and rage, mounting in his throat like blood, in his brain like fire, were yet not of such a kind as has vent in hot words; they were icy with the desolation of exiled death, as though he were drowning, and a ship passed, and none saw or heard him, and he raged against the ship.

The Judge was looking at him steadily, yet, it seemed to him, without communication, and he thought, as the drowning man of the steadfast, unrecognizing ship: if I can touch, I shall be safe; if I can be drawn in, I shall choke no longer in this besetting sea. His rage ebbed in an extreme weariness, and his courage sickened. A beggar's smile stiffened on his lips, and, edging nearer to the bed, he seated himself upon it and took Gaskony's arm.

"Let me do this," he said. "Don't ask why. Not for your sake, then—for mine. Let me do it for my sake!"

Gaskony released his arm. "If I took the money, Severidge, it would help neither you nor me. Don't think that, as far as I am concerned, I'm clinging to some barren asceticism or pluming myself on the virtue of poverty as such. If a bit more money came to me without setting up any kind of obligation— if I were to sell one or two of my chapters to a magazine, for example—I should take the money and be glad of it. It would ease things here, it would buy railway-tickets and help me to keep up one or two friendships I don't want to lose. And it would give me wine now and then, which I don't do without as easily as I do without smoke. . . . But I don't want to return to my former life. Not that it was a bad life; from many points of view it was a good one; I don't condemn it in myself—certainly not in others; but in fact it wasn't, for me, a creative life—it was just a pleasant existence. I loitered on from day to day, always finding some excuse for not writing the book that is—anyhow that might be—the one creative reason for my being in this planet at all. You will say I might have written it as well in the Temple as here. So I might, perhaps, if I'd been a different man. There's no magic about this place. There's no rule about conditions. But in practice no one does his life's work unless he first becomes the man who is fit to do it. No one runs a race unless he first goes into the training that suits him, and cuts out of his life the things that

[160]

impede him. So here I am—by no means Diogenes in his tub, but a man who has been forced back upon a way of living which enables him to do his life's work and which he never had the good sense or the courage to discover for himself. You think me rigid, no doubt. I am—in defence of what I have found."

Severidge straightened himself and rose. He ran his hands up the sides of his face and for a moment pressed his temples with his fingers. "I am sorry," he said. "I expect I have spoken extravagantly. I will go." He looked round the room. "I am confused to-night. At this moment, I seem scarcely to know who I am or why I am here."

"That is what I am learning," the Judge said.

"What?"

"Who I am—why I am here. There are receding answers to those questions. Gradually one comes up with them. It's like overtaking another traveller when you believe yourself lost. If I can overtake him, you think, he may be able to tell me my way home. You come nearer and nearer to him, and when you come up with him you see that he is yourself. There's still a long journey, but at least you have a companion. . . . I have put it clumsily," the Judge continued, "but it's the nearest I can come to explaining why I am happy as I am. Do you understand that that is true, Severidge? I am happy as I have never been."

"In your book?"

"Not even in my book. That may or may not be the flower of it. The root is in my life here—in myself, and beyond myself."

"Am I to believe that?"

"Is it so hard to believe?"

Severidge picked up a sheet of paper from the table and let it fall. "While you stand there, it is not hard to believe," he said reluctantly. Then wrath welled up in him again and he continued with biting vehemence: "But the more I believe that you are not lying, the less I bow down to your truth. The more I believe you, the more I hate and despise you. You are an accepter of life, I am a rebel against it. Why has man no courage? Why does he not rebel? The flower is always poisoned—do you never suspect the root? Even in Athens the flower was poisoned and died."

"Ah, Severidge," the Judge answered, standing at the open door with him, "it's not in Athens that you will teach me to despair. No one learns to hate life in the early morning."

"As far as human life is concerned," Severidge replied, "I make no distinction between morning and night."

"That is the answer of the dead."

At this Severidge, whose foot was on the stair, swung round, his eyes alight, but the words that sprang up in him were unspoken.

30

In Campion Road a thin rain was falling. As Severidge walked back it ceased, the wind dropped, but he did not notice the change. He walked with his hands clasped behind him and his head down, not taking in as a whole any street through which he passed, but moving stage by stage, curb by curb, lamp by lamp. He was engaged in a mental process of extreme violence: that of annihilating experience which denied his pleasure and threatened to frustrate his will.

It was necessary to destroy that little room, to wipe it from his mind—the tea-tray, the wall-paper, the slippery quilt, Gaskony's carved, rock-like head, his happiness and freedom; then to count the flagstones, and to touch this lamp-post and the next and the next, to feel the dripping iron cold against the back of his fingers; then to think of the lighted hotel, food and wine, the reflooding of the mind through the body, and to feel the flow of confidence, the lick of desire. It was his peculiarity, and a cause of his power over men, that he was able to induce in himself the unreason, or anti-reason, of a mob. While standing outside the mob and despising it, he could receive its heat into him and be inflamed by the self-intoxication of mass-thought. This enabled him to treat the world as his submissive instrument; it filled him with joyless gaiety, as though a mob were dancing in his mind.

In the hotel he engaged a room, ordered his suit-case to be brought in from his car, chose the Cheval Blanc they would drink at dinner—noting with satisfaction a price which suggested that the wine-list was unaware of its virtue—went upstairs, rang for a tray of drink, and bathed at leisure. Vivien, who had gone for a walk that had ended in darkness, was in the lounge not long before him. He told her that it was now too late to return to London; he didn't relish the long drive in the dark. Unless, of course, she had changed her mind and wished to return, he intended to stay the night.

"But you have nothing with you?"

"There's always a suit-case in the car for emergencies. I can stay very comfortably, unless, of course," he repeated, "you have changed your mind?"

"About seeing Gasky? Why should I?"

But he wished as yet to do no more than plant the doubt. "No particular reason," he said vaguely, implying that there was reason nevertheless. "You might have been thinking differently, that's all."

She asked how Gasky was.

"Do you know the place?" he said. "Wasn't the woman your old nurse?"

"Lou, yes. But I don't know her house. The last time I saw her was at my wedding. She came for it. Her husband was supposed to have come too, but he was ill. Soon afterwards he died and she moved. Is Gasky comfortable there? What is it like?"

"Modest," Severidge answered. "He's obviously economizing."

"In fact," Vivien said, "once he was on his own he always lived plainly. In London, and in the country when I was a child, he did himself pretty well in a modest way, but even that was chiefly convention, not personal choice. Position corresponded in his mind with a certain way of life; you didn't climb above it—that was showing off; you didn't simplify below it— that was showing off just as much; you lived about your own level, a bit more or a bit less, and weren't freakish. To be freakish was a bother—you had to explain it, and all Gasky cared about was to get his job done and have a chance to work at his *Athenian* in peace. He took the rest as it came—Rodd's and his cigars and so on—because it was the ordinary thing to do, not in the least because he was greedy for good living.

If we went off on a holiday we always lived without trappings in some little hotel or in lodgings—and that's what he likes inside him. He's a very solid but a very unpretentious Victorian—I think they were, the good ones, much less pretentious than we are." She was imagining sea-side lodgings to which the Judge had taken her—an unbeautiful but large front room with a balcony, another sitting-room as his den, a bedroom for him, a larger bedroom for her and her nurse—and she said: "I'm glad Lou has made him comfortable. I wondered sometimes, but I might have known she would. Your intelligence service seems to have been a bit off the track."

He smiled. "My intelligence service doesn't consist of unpretentious Victorians. They didn't know him as we know him. It was his resignation from Rodd's that worried me—unduly as it turns out. Still, he's living poorer than he did, as you'll see if you go. I asked him if I could do him a service, but he gave me more or less the answer of Diogenes: 'Yes, by standing out of the light'. That put poor Alexander in his place."

"He didn't mean to be unkind," Vivien said.

They went in to dinner together, laughing as they went. She had felt during her walk that, in leaving him as she did, she had been guilty not precisely of making a scene but of an impetuousness for which she must make amends. No amends were called for. Never was a man freer of that curse of mankind which she thought of as "forgiving hurtedness". He took her impetuousness in his stride, not recalling it even by hoping that she had reached home before dark or by sly reference to the little girl in the shelter—not recalling it at all, treating it as natural and charming because it was hers. Before his return she had been nervous, feeling that she had created a stress between them; she had been anxious, too, for Gasky, and lonely among the glass-lidded tables of the lounge and the electric chandeliers. Severidge, she had supposed, would return, give her a report on Gasky, drive off to London, and she would be stranded for the night, companionless among the illustrated papers and the ferns. Now she was not nervous for herself or anxious for

Gasky; there was no stress. Severidge talked good nonsense or good music—the two subjects that best pleased her on earth. There were oysters. As soon as she had tasted her Chablis, which was thin and sweet, she found that, opinion unasked, it was taken away and replaced by a very dry sherry. She enjoyed the invisible waving of wands.

"What really made you go to see Gasky at all?" she asked.

"You mean," he answered, "what business was it of mine? None, I suppose, strictly—except that he's one of the enviable men whom you happen to love." He paused long enough to let his words make their effect, but saved her the embarrassment of reply. "And I'll add the shameful confession," he went on, "that the Judge has always interested me more than I interest him. His is a friendship that I should enormously value."

"But you are friends—in a way."

" 'In a way'!" he repeated. "No, my dear, let's make no bones about it."

She asked: "Why his friendship particularly?"

"I will tell you," he said, speaking lightly but holding her eyes with direct challenge. "I should value his friendship for the same reason that I should value your love: it would change me. I want to be changed."

"I wonder," she said doubtfully, "or do you want to change others?"

"You might try," he answered.

Her face altered as though she had been sitting near a window and the lamp of a passing vehicle had shone into her eyes and pierced her. The change was momentary and scarcely physical—a vibration of her personality to be felt rather than observed. It was as if the shaft of light had passed through her like an invisible arrow. Severidge watched the impact, and the responsive glow; he asked no more as yet. This was not surrender—nothing but the interior glint of a traitor-light far off—but enough to set the mob dancing within him, shouting its invincibility. Her visible smile answered his fencingly as if to say: I know as well as you do that this is a game, not a battle, but her hand had moved on the table, and for an instant her lips had quivered with the beginning of a different smile, as though she were contemplating and recognizing a new face in her mirror.

He would not now press her further. They drank their Cheval Blanc and talked of music, a subject that entranced her always and stirred no alarm in her. Even her musical judgments had begun to take their colour from his. When he disparaged Chopin, who had been among her personal gods, her reply was almost apologetic, a defence not a bold claim. For the delight of seeing how plastic her judgments had become, how he could shape them to his suggestion as if they had been clay under his hand, he quoted against himself Tolstoy's exclamation after listening to a prelude of Chopin's: "That is the kind of short story one ought to write!" At once her pleasure in Chopin revived, but when he said that the nocturnes were falsely sentimental and that much of the so-called passionate music was rhetoric for the fashionable drawing-rooms of another age, she was shaken and almost consented. Then he reminded her again of Tolstoy's view. Mozart, Tolstoy had said, was sometimes empty, and Schubert's fault was virtuosity, but Chopin, however simple he might be, was never empty, and in his most complicated works was never a mere virtuoso. "That is true," Vivien exclaimed at once. "That is what I have always felt," but it was easy to sway her opinion back again. Chopin was for her a true master, he spoke to her inmost self, he supplied her integrity; yet she could be made to deny him; and Severidge thought: there will soon be nothing of herself that she will not deny, her self will cease to exist.

The surrender of her body might, or might not, be a step towards the surrender of her mind. This was unimportant to him. What he desired was possession more far-reaching than possession of the body, and he foresaw how, gradually, he would separate her from her own loyalties—from Chopin; from Henry who would become more and more his obsequious creature, the ardent slave of the Severidge Foundation; and from Gaskony, whom she loved. Through her, he could reach

Gaskony still; in his love for her the old man was still vulnerable; disaster to her would break up even *The Athenian*. He saw how, isolated, she would cease to have any being except as a subject of his domination, a part of the mob dancing within his mind, and, though he knew that in the end she must go to Campion Road, he wished to postpone her meeting with Gaskony so that it might not be associated with himself in her thought. Therefore, when dinner was over and coffee had been brought to them in the lounge, he spoke of their return to London next day. Would ten o'clock be too early a start?

"But you must not wait for me," she said. "I have to see Gasky."

"If you still intend to."

"But why not? I came for that."

"That was my fault. My intelligence service gave a false alarm."

"Even so, now that I am here——"

"Well," he said, "that's for you to decide. I thought that you might not wish to bother him."

As he had intended, she caught at the word.

" 'Bother'?" she said, hearing an echo of Gasky's voice.

"Isn't it a kind of family catchword?"

"Did he speak to you of that?"

"In passing."

"Are you trying to tell me that Gasky doesn't want to see me?"

"My dear Vivien, he said nothing of the kind."

"But did he say, speaking of me, that—I mean, was it when you were speaking of me that he told you about the family catchword? Between him and me that means a lot, you know."

"I know it does. That's why I told you."

"Very well," she answered. "Then I will drive back with you at ten o'clock to-morrow morning."

She became silent and distraught. When she spoke, it was from a mind preoccupied. Once more she was seeing herself as she had when she was walking on Severidge's arm to visit

Gasky. Why am I doing this? It is unlike me. She was failing to recognize herself in the girl sitting with Severidge at a glass-lidded table, assenting to his judgments, excited by his company, and now, suddenly, afraid to visit Gasky—excluded, it seemed, by Gasky himself. She glanced at Severidge, straightened herself in her chair and drew breath, intending to ask again what Gasky really had said, but Severidge was talking of Mozart's special use of G minor, she was answering him and was afraid to put her question. He would think it unreasonable and ridiculous that she should return to the subject, and a voice within her, seemingly her own, began to persuade her that, in reason, her anxiety, her sense of losing grip, of being isolated and adrift, was ridiculous. She felt again as she had when her arm had been enclosed in his and he was urging her forward, away from herself, into the desert. Her will slipping, only intuition remained. It surged in her—a wild desire to be free, to be out of the mob, to escape from chaos into order. So she rose and left him.

He sat at the table with his finger-tips pressed together, his lips slightly pouting, and his eyes sidelong for her return. When she came back he would rise and move her chair six inches. She would sit down, he too, and, as he began to speak, her eyes would come up to his and she would smile. But she did not return. He waited a long time, then went to her bedroom and knocked. There was no answer. He inquired at the desk. Her key was on the rack. The porter said that the lady, wearing a raincoat, had gone out some time ago. Severidge returned to the chair he had previously occupied. He was pale with anger and continually thrust a finger between his throat and the collar of his shirt. After a little while, he went for his own overcoat, then to the garage. He drove slowly at first, thinking he might overtake her, but there were many side-streets by which she might have gone, and he pressed down the accelerator, determined, if he could, to be at Campion Road before her. As the time of waiting lengthened and she did not come, he understood that he had missed her; she was with the Judge now. He let the car glide away from the house, turned the corner, stopped and got out. He would wait for her on foot. One of the windows in Number Eight was fully lighted and uncurtained. The people within appeared and vanished, appeared and vanished. They seemed to be playing some game. Remembering that he must be visible in the window-beam, he moved away down the street, and began to walk to and fro, keeping Number Eight in sight and touching the fluted iron of the lamp-posts with the back of his fingers.

31

"AND now?" Vivien was saying. "What now? Is it going to be a great book, Gasky? You probably know inside you by now."

He was in bed, propped against pillows. The block of paper on which he had been writing when she entered lay on the coverlet among sheets already used and torn off, and she was in the small armchair, drawn up beside him. That he might be warm with the gas-fire turned low he had gone to bed after supper, and so she had found him, working, when Lou, having welcomed her in the kitchen, had at last consented to take her upstairs. Even then Lou had so evidently been reluctant to go that the Judge had made her sit down with them. She had talked not much, but had kept her eyes on Vivien as though it were still a delightful puzzle to her that the girl she saw and whose voice she heard should be, and yet should not be, the little girl she had known. Soon she asked for a promise that she should see Vivien again—"and for a real talk, mind you, not just a hug and good-bye"—and, given this promise, she said good-night, as she always had in the past, unhurryingly, step by step withdrawing, good-night, good-night, until the last good-night was said round a half-closed door.

"Well," the Judge had said when she was gone, "you have caught me in the act, Vivien, my dear! This is cards on the table." He had told her briefly of the circumstances in which he had come to be poor, and she, in turn, had told of Henry's increasing prosperity and of how she had driven down from London with Severidge that day. Neither had cross-examined the other. Even in Vivien's childhood, the essence of their relationship had been a respect for each other's independence—

you did not ask for attention or for confidences—and the rule held. Neither had ever been afraid of, or even embarrassed by, the other. There was, therefore, a natural frankness between them, and Gaskony could say without modest pretence or boasting that *The Athenian* would make good use of unrivalled material. He believed, he added, that, though as the years went by a part of his material must be superseded, the book, on its merits, would stand the test of time.

"Then you are doing what you wanted to do?"

"Odd thing is," he said, "I feel like a young man writing his first book—it's as exciting as that—and yet I don't feel the young man's uncertainty about what I'm aiming at. I know the statue inside the block of marble as if I could touch it with my hands. To cut it out is a different matter. I haven't the sureness in prose which comes, I take it, with unremitting practice—so that the chisel becomes part of your hand. Sentence by sentence, I'm getting control. Even the paragraphs are becoming less stubborn. It's the transitions that worry me—one line of thought or of character growing into another—but there's always the waste-paper basket if only you have the courage to use it. Then there's the other kind of courage—*not* to use it hastily because you're tired and it seems easier to destroy than to revise."

She knew already so much of *The Athenian*, for she had grown up in its climate, that to her he could talk of it by reference; she could interpret its progress and relate its triumphs and struggles to the whole design. When he said that he was happy and now felt himself to be alive as he had never been, she had no need to ask why.

"What interested me in Severidge," he said, "was his point of view. First he wanted to rescue me. When I said no, he made up his mind that my living here was asceticism for the sake of asceticism. He had the notion that I was afraid of life and was running away from it. You might as well say that a man who chose to live in the country was 'afraid' of the life of cities, or that one who chose to be a doctor was 'afraid' of being a barrister. People who speak of being 'afraid of life' think of it in terms of quantity and mass; they forget its quality and variety. When I was at school we used to drive out to cricket matches in wagonettes. We hung over the side and scorned the passers-by; I think we pitied them, poor devils, because they weren't enjoying themselves as we were and weren't singing our choruses, but had to walk while we bowled along in company. It didn't occur to us that walking, too, could be a lively activity. Your Mr. Severidge is still in the wagonette."

"My Mr. Severidge?"

The dart of criticism came to her from him so rarely that she flinched. At once, with a smile, he tried to unbarb it.

"No," she said, "don't withdraw, Gasky. I'm in a mess, though it's hard to describe. The fact that I am here at all, with him, describes it better than words can."

She told him of her walk with Severidge along the front that afternoon and of her refusal when they had been about to turn in towards Campion Road; she described their talk of the Severidge Foundation and of Henry's part in it; and last she told how, after dinner, she had almost consented not to come to Campion Road at all, and, suddenly, had come.

"Do you like him, Vivien?"

"Like?" she repeated.

"Or admire?"

"Neither 'like' nor 'admire', and yet—you'll have to find another word, Gasky."

"I'd rather wait until you find it."

"He's a steel that strikes a spark out of my flint," she answered.

"But you aren't flint, my dear."

"I know. He puts that into me first. It's strange now, looking back—at dinner I ran down Chopin."

"Not much spark in that," said the Judge.

"Isn't there? Lies, too, glitter sometimes. Besides, I half-believed what I said."

"Do you still?"

She looked at him—the long, keen face, the calm eyes, the hands outspread on the coverlet. "Not here. Not now."

"But when you get back to—to that hotel or to London——"

"Then," she said, "God knows, I might half-believe anything. Oh, it's such a relief to be here, Gasky! You, sitting there with your *Athenian*—you are like someone looking out of a fortress at the hosts of Midian. Your fortress isn't mine, I know; everyone has his own if he can find it; but any rate you make me feel that I have one, and that life isn't an anonymous, meaningless drift. I'm not alone in feeling that and hating it," she added when he moved to interrupt her. "Isn't half the world in the same kind of mess, wanting to have spark struck out of it by one form of enthusiasm or another? He makes me feel like a mob, marching in step, excited, confident, bands playing, all worked up. It's a hot feeling. . . . What am I to do—cut him out? Say I won't ever see him again?" The Judge did not answer and she continued: "If I do, then where am I? All I shall have done is make a selfish, hysterical scene, and spoil Henry's chances just when he has begun to build them up. I believe, for instance, that the Severidge Foundation is pitch, but, after all, that's only my opinion. One evening last November Henry and I went for a walk along the Embankment together. There was some question at the time of his going to Stockholm with Severidge. He was worried—not by that only—he was worried about us, and he asked me a question which—anyhow I avoided it; I didn't really answer it at all. But that's a long story. . . . Now, it's really the same question again. Am I to tell Henry not to touch the Severidge business—persuade him out of it?"

"I shouldn't persuade him to do or not do anything," the Judge said. "There's too much persuasion in the world—righteous as well as unrighteous. For the same reason, I'm not going to try to persuade you."

There was a long silence. "Do you remember," Vivien said, "an afternoon when you came to the Red House and we had tea outside together and——"

"There were many afternoons that tally with that pleasant description."

"It was Mother's birthday. You gave me this diamond clip."

"I remember well."

"You were frightened about Severidge then. Yes, Gasky, you were—just as I am now. . . . And now, here, in this room you are not. You never will be again. . . . But I can't come to live in lodgings. I haven't a great book to write."

"It's not a question of its being a great book," Gaskony answered. "It's my own book. It's myself. That's the point."

Vivien took his pen from the table. "I am half afraid of thinking about myself, myself, myself. I'm tired of saying: 'What shall I do?' when all the answers contradict one another. You forget," she added, "I haven't a book at all."

"Nonsense," he said.

"Are you suggesting that I should learn to write?"

"No," he answered abruptly. "That you should learn to be. Learn that and nothing can touch you, neither authoritarianism nor the devil himself." He came up from his pillows and leaned forward, pointing across the room with arm outstretched. "Give me that book, Vivien. Fourth shelf; third from the left." When she had handed it to him, he leaned back again, slowly finding the place. He drew the lamp towards him and held the page in its ring. "Listen," he said. "This is Eve speaking to Adam. Do you remember? She wants to go off on her own, thinking she's safe enough. Listen:

> How are we happy, still in fear of harm?
> But harm precedes not sin: only our foe
> Tempting affronts us with his foul esteem
> Of our integrity: his foul esteem
> Sticks no dishonour on our front, but turns
> Foul on himself. . . .

Under-estimate the foe. Split your integrity. Divide your forces. Consequences always the same," the Judge said, "on the battlefield or in Paradise."

Vivien smiled at his vehemence. "I remember your saying that afternoon that your poor friend Severidge hadn't a cloven hoof. I think it's true. He's often kind and good. I think he's honestly fond of me—and of you."

[175]

"May be. Sometimes," the Judge answered, turning two
pages of the book in his hands, "but listen again:

> That space the Evil One abstracted stood
> From his own evil, and for the time remained
> Stupidly good, of enmity disarmed,
> Of guile, of hate, of envy, of revenge.
> But the hot hell that always in him burns,
> Though in mid-Heaven, soon ended his delight,
> And tortures him now more, the more he sees
> Of pleasure not for him ordained. Then soon
> Fierce hate he recollects. . . .

That's the authoritarian ebb and flow since the beginning of
time. Milton noticed it in Satan. More discreet about Crom-
well."

Vivien hesitated. "Gasky," she said. "I'm muddled and tired.
For you, Milton's a short cut to what you are trying to say.
But I—well, I understand it with my mind. First: don't divide
your forces, as Eve did. Second: beware of the devil when he's
gentle and wise. . . . I understand it. But, put in that way, it
doesn't help me now. Tell me, not in Milton's words but in
your own, what I am to do."

" 'What I am to be'," the Judge said, correcting her.

"What I am to be. Who I am," she answered. "Tell me in
your own words." As he did not at once answer and because
her eyes were filling with tears, she stood at the mantelpiece and
looked at the little Sickert hanging there.

"If I say what I think," the Judge said in a low, reluctant
voice, "it can be no more than what I think—and the life in
question is your life. That is why I let Milton speak—so that
it might be you, you yourself, who interpreted him. It has
always been a pact between us two, Vivien, that we shouldn't
bother each other. If that means that we should not interfere
with each other's actions, how much more that we should
not—" he gathered the coverlet under his fingers, "that we
should not tread upon each other's souls. It's seldom worth
doing, particularly across the generations."

"But you are my father," she said.

He drew in his breath with a gasp of pain. "Ah, if that were true——"

"You are my father and my mother," she said.

To this he gave no answer. His hands moved up and lay, frail and bony, across the open pages of his Milton. His head was inclined forward. "Then I will speak," he said, "and, because I am old and a man I pray that your mother may speak in me." He raised his head, looked unwaveringly at the girl before him, and began:

"You say to me that I am your father, but, Vivien, I am neither your father in the flesh nor your father in God. I have no right in you except my love, if love gives right. So far as any human love may be, mine for you is, I believe, selfless and absolute." At this, his confidence shook. He gave a little shrug of his shoulders as though to surrender the claim upon her that he had just made, and added: "It's as if a child were to come to me and ask: 'Who is God?'—to *me*! How can I answer?" His lips closed and tightened as he fortified himself against misgiving. "Well," he exclaimed, "you have set me a summing-up!"

But for a long time no words came. He had begun to meditate the discourse he would deliver, an extremely subtle and, he hoped, a persuasive discourse, but his eye fell upon the colour and curve of her cheek and he said to himself: Bless my soul, this isn't a philosophical student, this is a girl damn near to making a fool of herself. No good preaching at her. But no good, either, patting her shoulder and playing down. She's no fool. She has asked the hardest question in the world, the question on which all others depend—who am I?—but she has had the sense to ask it. Has to be answered somehow. No good saying: be a good girl, stick to your own man. Has to be answered. But she must be made to answer it for herself. And he saw that what was required of him was not a summing-up but an examination-in-chief—a bit of cross-examination, too, perhaps. I must climb down off the Bench, he thought; I must go back to the Bar.

"Vivien," he said.

"Yes, Gasky."

"The question is—isn't it?—whether what you are looking for really exists."

" 'Myself'?"

"Yourself, yes, but at what level? how deep? Obviously not your name or the colour of your cheeks or your voice. Or would you say that what you are looking for is what you feel yourself to be at this moment of this particular evening?"

"No, that isn't what I mean."

"Or what you have felt yourself to be to-day, or this week, or this year?"

"I don't think it has much to do with time," she said.

"Nor with appearances or behaviour? They are the glint and ripple on the surface of the stream, and what you are looking for is something deeper than that. Does it exist? Can you say what it is?"

Her lips moved but she was silent.

"Is it what we call 'conscience'?"

She shook her head. "I don't think so. Conscience, which in me is a pretty swerving beast anyway, may be one of its results."

" 'A swerving beast'?"

"Shies at ghosts," she said with a smile. "Doesn't like long hills. Can't forget her comfortable stable."

"Ah," the Judge answered, "it's not only your voice that's like your mother's. But she took the hills, nevertheless. . . . Then," he continued, "the thing you are looking for isn't your conscience or your appearances and behaviour—can you say yet what it is? Just now, when I asked the same question, your lips moved. What were you going to say?"

"You'd think it stupid, Gasky—stupid, I mean, as applied to me."

"Why?"

"Well," she said, "perhaps not. You always said he 'applied'—Plato, I mean. Do you remember teaching me that bit of the Symposium in which he says that, at the heart of beautiful things, there is Absolute Beauty? Even he can't say in words what it *is*. And I——"

"No, no. Stop!" the Judge exclaimed. "Don't shy away from that hill. Listen. If there is a principle of beauty at the heart of beautiful things, and a principle of life at the heart of living things, would you not say that there is a principle of individuality—an essence without which you would not be—at the heart of your individuality?"

"Yes," she answered.

"There is an Absolute You as there is an Absolute Beauty?"

"I think so."

"Then," he cried, "when you say 'Who am I?' isn't it this that you are seeking?"

"Certainly it is, Socrates," she answered, challenging his eagerness with a flash of delighted amusement. "That is what I should have said if you hadn't interrupted me. I got there a little sooner than you did."

He threw himself back against his pillows, laughing with her. "That may be. That may be," he exclaimed. "I've always believed that Socrates was taught by his pupils. But he led them into teaching him—don't you forget that."

His laughter and her smiling mockery of him by the name of Socrates was a signal across the years. So she had mocked him in the past when he had tried to teach her by the hard questioning of the Socratic method, drawing her into a corner where, suddenly, she must teach herself. This she had forgotten, he also, but now they remembered it, and the remembrance lifted the screen which, for all their continuing affection, had grown up since her marriage between their distinct lives. They were together again, and she began to recognize herself as she had been before confusion fell upon her and to feel again the singleness of her girlhood that had been confirmed and deepened, in a way that Gasky had at first found hard to understand, during the early years of her marriage.

When his voice sounded again in her thought, she listened, giving all her mind to his argument, but she was no longer dependent on him; her own strength was returning to her from a source within herself, and she listened as she had in her child-hood to a familiar story—held by it the more closely because she knew its end.

A man, he was saying, might be thought of as a wheel. The centre of a revolving wheel was a point, it had position but no magnitude; the true centre of a revolving wheel didn't revolve, the wheel revolved about it.

"Of course," Gasky said, "the ordinary, practical observer—the chap, I mean, who is interested in nothing except to watch the wheels go round—would probably say that that was hair-splitting. Let him say. The world's in the devil's own mess chiefly because it has forgotten that some hairs have to be split. Still, let's give the practical man a chance. He would say that because he—no, he'd say, bless his superstitious eyes, that because Science couldn't measure the centre of a wheel, the centre didn't exist—for practical purposes. He'd say that a wheel consists in its appearances—the hub, the spokes, the rim; and probably, if he was a sound utilitarian, he'd add that its effective part was its rim, which alone was in contact with the earth or with the driving-band or what you will. Can you answer him?"

"I can guess how you would answer him."

"How?"

"Take the wheel to bits and ask questions about them."

"Well," said the Judge, "you can laugh at me, but isn't it common sense? If I took away a part of the rim, or some of the spokes, or even the hub, wouldn't you still say the thing was a wheel?"

"If they were still recognizable."

"And what would make them recognizable as a wheel? What else," he demanded with the leap of a hound coming up with his quarry, "what else than their convergence on the centre? *They* can all go hang; the wheel may be broken, but it can continue to exist without any one of them. But nothing is more inconceivable than a wheel without a centre. The centre—not the hub or the spokes or the rim—is the thing with-out which a wheel is not. So your innermost being isn't your character, which may be likened to a wheel's spokes, or your actions which are its rim, or even your observable personality which may be thought of as a wheel's hub; it is that upon which they all depend; it is that without which you are not. It is that being which tells you of the single origin of all beings, of the single law governing all laws, of the single value from which all values spring. You can't describe it. I know that. Socrates couldn't. Jesus himself spoke in parables. But you are continuously aware of it. For years you may not ask: 'Who am I?' Men go all their lives without asking a question about the circulation of their blood. But there is never a time, waking or sleeping, in which the idea 'I am' is not alive in you, unaffected by time, deeper than thought, deeper than feeling, the very spring of instinct and intuition, the original, the unsilenceable whisper of the soul."

When he had said this, the Judge frowned and shut his eyes; then opened them wide. "There it is. . . . There it is," he said, dividing sentence from sentence as he did always when embarrassed. "Sorry, my dear. Talking beyond myself. As if I had authority. Believe me, I claim none. Tell me. Do you still love that rascal of yours?"

"Henry? Yes, Gasky."

"I don't mean 'in love'. I take it that continues. Am I right?"

"Yes."

"Well, then, the other? What was it—apart from biological chemistry—made you love him at all? Him and no other?"

"Something I recognized," she said. "Not the spokes of the wheel, Gasky. It's centre, perhaps. I thought so, anyhow."

"And now? What happened—well, when one or two of the spokes broke?"

"He's mending them. Give him credit."

"I do give him credit. I like your rascal. . . . But what happened to you?"

Vivien leaned back with her hands clasped behind her head. "I know the answer. But oh—it would take me half my life to tell you."

"As long as you know the answer," he said. "That's all I

want. . . . You see, Vivien," he continued, "for me, who have known you all your life, you are always essentially the same unique person. Whatever you did or became would make no odds. That absolute identity persists, though you have grown up and though your face and your manners and even what we call your character change. It's as if the centre of the wheel—the soul, if you like—had a recognizable voice, and I take it you also think it has; if you didn't, Henry's adventure in the markets would have made nonsense of your marriage long ago. Anyhow, you have a recognizable voice for me. Dare say, being outside you, I hear it faintly; sometimes, being an old curmudgeon, dare say I hear it wrong. But it's inside you. You can hear it all right if you listen. Can't you?"

"Rather dim sometimes, Gasky. Or rather—" she hesitated "—not exactly dim but like an actor saying a part. Horribly convincing, but not his own words—someone else's. It was like that this evening when I ran down Chopin. That was flat contrary to my own intelligence and yet, while I said it, it seemed to come from inside me. It wasn't insincere."

"My God, but you aren't your intelligence!" he exclaimed. This was the first time that there had been allusion to Severidge, and the Judge, resisting his first angry impulse, avoided the name. "You are your whole self—the infant you have forgotten, the child you remember, the old woman you will be. You are the girl who saw that life was good, believed it with a single heart, and began to doubt it with a divided intellect. You learned, as we all do, that, taking it all in all, there is more suffering than happiness in experience, and then I suppose, being a child of your age, you decided that, if only we were clever enough, we might by our sole intelligence redress the balance between happiness and suffering. It doesn't work. It might if evil were outside our intelligence, but it isn't. That's why you hear the actor saying his part. That's why we can all lie against ourselves without being what is called 'insincere'. Evil isn't an army that besieges a city from outside the walls. It is native of the city. It's the mutiny in the garrison, the poison in the water, the ashes in the bread."

She said: "I know." Then she looked over her shoulder towards the door. "I wish he would come," she said.

"Who?"

"Henry."

"Are you expecting him?"

"No. All the same, he might come—except, of course, he has no address for me. But he could come here." She sat rigidly, her head turned, watching the handle of the door. "It doesn't matter," she said, turning back. "It's as if he had."

She covered her face, but her shoulders did not move; she was not crying, and Gaskony waited. Suddenly she took down her hands, put her arms about him, and laid her cheek against his.

"My dear," he said, "ask yourself in what work, what company, what loyalty your own voice is clear and in what muffled. By the answer, rule your life. You have only to listen. God is not dumb."

When she had released him, he put his hand against his cheek, gathering in all the years of his life and the glory of their not having cheated him. He had felt, as she held him, the shudder of her safety, as though his child had run into his arms.

Not his words only, but the steadiness of him had given her peace. She watched him now, upright in his bed, Milton in his hands, his eyes alight with his thought, and was no longer afraid or entangled. It was not that she had found answers to all the questions that had beset her, but that the questions themselves were becoming transparent, like a mist pierced by the sun. She made no plan of action except that she would telephone to Henry before she slept that night, if he had not by then found her as she half believed that he would. What words she would use she did not know, but she knew that he also would sleep peacefully.

The Judge stretched out his hand. "You are tired, my dear. You are swaying on your feet. Come, say good-night to me. Your Henry will walk home with you, whether in fact he's here or not."

She smiled at that and came nearer. "When you read me

the Odyssey," she said, "there was a piece you made me learn. You said it was your piece. I wondered why. Now I know."

"Your mother found it for me," he answered. "Say it."

" 'Then the sun set,' " she repeated, " 'and they came to the famous grove, the sacred place of Athene; so there the goodly Odysseus sat him down . . . and Pallas Athene heard him, but she did not yet appear to him face to face.' "

"Not yet," the Judge said and took her hand. She stooped and kissed him and went out.

In the street, she raised her face to the wind, and Severidge saw her face, and fell back and let her go.

The Judge climbed out of his bed and set his table in readiness for the morning. When all was done, he turned out his lamp and lay down, thinking of Nausicaa. "This was the last word of the tale, when sweet sleep came speedily upon him . . . unknitting the cares of his soul."

ZENNOR—LONDON
March 1945–September 1946